A VIOLENT SHOCK . . .

The red glow of the fire sufficiently illuminated the room for Anna to see the man who had saved her life. She looked at him with grateful curiosity, only to sway on her feet, her heart thudding in panic, as she recognized him.

Her rescuer was Charles Baccoult.

Recalling his violence when they first met, she could not relax. But he made no move to touch her, and she looked at him critically. In the glare of the shadows his face was all dark hollows and stark angles. The sardonic black eyes, arrogant long nose, and strong jaw magnetized the eye. He was someone to arouse both fear and awe. Such violence combined with such gentleness was rare in a man.

Sheila Holland
SHADOWS AT DAWN

PLAYBOY PRESS
PAPERBACKS

Published simultaneously in the United States and Canada by Playboy Press, Chicago, Illinois. Printed in the United States of America. Library of Congress Catalog Card Number: 79-84690. Originally published in Great Britain in 1975 by Robert Hale & Company.

Books are available at quantity discounts for promotional and industrial use. For further information, write our sales promotion agency: Ventura Associates, 40 East 49th Street, New York, New York 10017.

ISBN: 0-872-16535-3

First Playboy Press softcover printing September 1979.

One

Paris, in the late summer of 1793, was a nightmare world, where death shimmered in the early morning heat haze rising off the Seine, and hatred and suspicion ran like pestilence through the streets. They had pulled down the ancient walls of the city to allow expansion, and built broad new boulevards where the fashionable could stroll in comfort, but the narrow, winding streets in the inner core were much as they had been in the Middle Ages, dark, dirty and stinking of human refuse. Crowded tenements overhung the streets, their gables almost touching, creaking in the wind like anchored galleons. Their inhabitants, red-eyed like sewer rats, carried the infection of their breeding in their surly faces.

These were the people who had seized upon the revolution in a frenzy of terrible joy, believing it to be the beginning of a new world for themselves and their children.

But the dazzling vista of freedom was receding now, and the present, by contrast, seemed to them more unbearable than ever.

All over Paris men were awakening from a dream

of splendor to realize that they still went hungry to bed, still wore foul rags and lived in poverty and filth. The promise of happiness had proved illusory.

The other nations of Europe threatened them. Bread was scarce and expensive. Rumor and counterrumor set the city in a blaze of constant suspicion.

Like terrified animals, they grew daily more savage, snarling at every shadow that moved in the darkness around them. Their long oppression had made them angry. Fear made them cruel. And the new government, nervous for its own safety, used the time-honored trick of driving out a scapegoat. They blamed all that went wrong upon the interference of foreign governments, and the people turned furiously upon anyone who had foreign blood.

It was dangerous to be a foreigner in Paris in that long, hot summer of 1793.

There were, as there have always been, small colonies of English visitors in Paris, and in one of these, in a decaying lodging house in the Rue de Vernueil, a young Frenchman was kneeling beside a brocade chaise lounge, his handsome, olive-skinned face turned upward in pleading.

"Marie," he breathed, trying to seize one of the small, white hands which played restlessly with a gilded fan. "Marie, *je t'aime . . .*"

"Citizen Baccoult," replied the young lady in a distinct English accent, "you should not say that!" Her French was lisping, and she drawled, and he found it adorable.

"But I do," he insisted, flushing. He was twenty, very uncertain of himself, despite what his mirror must tell him, and this was his first affair of the heart. Eager, passionate, idealistic, he knew no more of women than of flying to the moon.

She gave him a contemptuous glance from behind her fan. "And my name is Maria, not Marie!" she corrected, adding, "but you must not use it! If my Papa should hear you, he would be very angry!"

He cast an alarmed look at the door. "He will be shocked to find you here alone with me?"

She shrugged. "Anna will warn us if my father returns early!"

He looked blank.

"My cousin," she reminded him, her eyes amused, and patted the cushions beside her. "You look so tall, standing there! You make me feel helpless."

He sank down beside her, trembling slightly, his black eyes hot with passion. "When you look up at me your eyes are like blue stars," he murmured on a caught breath.

Her lashes fluttered rapidly, the pink lips parting in eager enjoyment. Compliments delighted her. She gave him a smile, encouraging him to continue.

He swallowed hard. "Your skin is as white as the petals of that rose," and he touched tentatively the flower she wore pinned in the fichu of her gown.

She lay back, her blue eyes inviting. Head swimming, he bent until his lips touched the enchanting whiteness of her throat. She could hear the heavy thud of his heart, his quickened breathing.

"La, sir!" she exclaimed after a moment, sitting up and fanning herself vigorously. "You go too far! When I conceded this private interview I did not suspect you intended such impudence!"

In the black eyes a tiny, flickering flame died out. With burning cheeks, he begged her to forgive him. "I lost my head! It will not happen again!"

After some persuasion, she agreed to forgive him, and changed the subject. "You will attend our salon tonight? We expect Feuvielle."

As she had expected, the name brought a wild flash from his dark eyes. "That aristo! Why do you torment me by encouraging him? It drives me mad to see you in his company day after day! You are too innocent to know what manner of man he is, but I have warned you of his reputation before! Why do you not believe me?"

"My Papa thinks highly of him. I have heard he is a force in government circles, and certainly he is a fervent republican! He renounced his title long ago!"

"I do not trust him! I am convinced he is in secret league with the royalists. There is an insolence about him which stamps him as one of them. The very way he smiles is an insult."

She watched him from beneath her pale, thick lashes with secret amusement. "Of course, it could not be that you are jealous of him?"

He gazed at her with uncertain longing, and she laughed. "You do not need to answer!" she teased.

Louis began to stammer hotly, but before he had said more than two words the door opened, and he sprang to his feet in confusion.

"My uncle is on the stairs," said the newcomer coldly.

Louis retreated, with a last passionate glance, and Maria Campbell sank back upon her cushions, purring like a cat. Her cousin, Anna, looked across the room at her with stifled irritation.

"This is the last time you use me as a cover for your indiscretions, Maria!"

Her attitude one of sensual relaxation, Maria laughed. "La, Miss! You are jealous because you cannot get yourself a handsome Frenchman!"

"I think you should not encourage the young man when you know very well you do not mean to have him!"

"He amuses me," dismissed Maria; then, sharply, "and hold your tongue, Miss! Why should I not encourage him if I please? I do not intend to marry the first handsome young man I meet, but I see no reason why I should live like a nun! It is dull enough in Paris, heaven knows! With Papa forever talking politics, and most of the men so dull and stuffy! Revolution seems to be as boring as Papa's charity work in London!"

"You will hurt him quite appallingly," said Anna, her blue eyes dark with concern.

Maria looked across the room with complacence. Anna was tall and slender, looking in her plain white muslin, like a schoolgirl, her thick chestnut hair simply dressed on the nape of her neck, one soft curl twining down into the bosom of her gown. Her eyes were gentle and serious, a darker blue than Maria's, and softer. Beside Maria's diminutive prettiness, Anna looked almost clumsy.

"Why are you so anxious, Miss? Do you want him for yourself?"

She watched maliciously as Anna flushed crimson.

"What nonsense!" Anna retorted.

"Oh," purred Maria, settling down to enjoy herself. "It would be an excellent match for you, no doubt! But, my poor Anna, he would not even look at you."

"I am sorry for him," Anna cried, her pride stung. "I have seen you playing with young men, Maria. Like a cat with a bird. Why do you not be content with Feuvielle? He, at least, knows what game it is you are playing. He is a practiced flirt. Louis is not."

Maria fluttered her lashes. "Louis! You use his name, I see. Poor Anna, I am sorry for you! When I mentioned your name to him he did not even recall you!" And with a spiteful smile she whisked herself out of the room before Anna could take breath to reply.

Anna stamped her feet in a sudden gust of temper, then laughed at herself for being provoked. For, after all, it was untrue that she had any interest in young Louis Baccoult, and it was foolish to allow Maria to tease her.

She went to her own room, changed into a spotted pink silk which did very little for her, eyed her reflection with regret and went back to the salon, where she found her uncle reading the evening paper.

She kissed the top of his head, noting that his hair was growing very thin, and he smiled vaguely at her.

Anna was nineteen, the daughter of a Scots army officer who had died when she was small. Her mother had returned to her own home, taking Anna with her, and in a quiet Kent village Anna had lived until she was twelve, when a typhoid epidemic deprived her of her mother and grandparents at once.

She had been taken to her uncle's house in London, to be a companion to his own daughter, Maria, a year her senior. Arriving lost, lonely and bewildered, she had been greeted by her uncle, Sir Henry Campbell, with a warm hug. Sandy-haired, sturdy and hot-tempered, he was so much like her dimly remembered father that she had felt as though she had, indeed, found her own Papa again.

Having been brought up by a household of women, Anna naturally enjoyed this new relationship. The sound of a deep masculine voice, the indulgent kindness of a male towards young females, delighted her, and apart from all this her uncle rapidly won her deep respect for his own character.

His brusque manner, she found, hid a kind heart, much worked upon by the misery around him. From his sense of pity grew strong radical opinions. He worked in London for the ending of slavery, and sat on the boards of charitable institutions of all kinds. A never-ending stream of food, clothes, money went out from his home to those in need. His servants grumbled, his relations complained, but Sir Henry was deaf. Yet he felt that this piecemeal way of mending the ills of the world would not answer. "If a tree is rotten we chop it down and burn it," he would say angrily. "It does no good to lop a branch here, a branch there. The tree of society is in a parlous state!"

When the revolution broke out in France he was so excited that with typical impulsive haste he moved himself and his family there, and at once became involved in many activities in Paris, both commercial and political. He had always had business interests in France, but those now trebled, and he declared his intention of remaining there forever.

Maria he had most thoroughly spoiled. His wife had died at her birth, and he had showered the pretty, delicate child with love. He thought her an angel, and Maria took good care that he should never catch her in one of her more disagreeable moods. Always sunny and sweet with her father, Maria never bothered to try to impress Anna. She cared little for women's opinion, and even less for those of a poor relation. She constantly reminded Anna of her dependent position, but was careful never to push her cousin too far, for, in truth, Maria found Anna useful. She took the household duties upon herself, leaving Maria free to amuse herself.

Over recent months, Anna suspected that her uncle had grown disillusioned with the revolution. The trend in the course of events was all too plain. The bloody massacres which had broken out in the last year had horrified him. Yet, when Maria begged him to return to England, Anna remained silent. She knew him well enough to know that advice usually resulted in forcing him to an opposite viewpoint. Sir Henry was a stubborn, difficult man. Anna hoped that his love for his daughter would persuade him where volumes of common sense did not.

Maria now appeared for dinner, an enchanting picture in the tight-waisted, full-skirted blue silk gown. Her golden ringlets fell around her tiny, heart-shaped face, and her cheeks had a soft flush as she kissed her father. He looked at her with tender delight, hardly believing that he had produced such a beauty.

They had one guest for dinner that evening, a lawyer from Dijon whose quiet manners hid a shrewd mind. Sir Henry and he had business dealings, and throughout the meal the topic was entirely centered upon the economy of the country, while Maria pouted and twined a curl around her finger, sulky that the lawyer should seem so indifferent to her charms.

The maid who waited on them was slow and clumsy. Maria flashed her a furious glance as she spilled a basket of rolls in taking them from the table. "Be careful, girl! Really, Anna, the servants are impossible!"

Anna, looking at the maid, saw her large eyes cloud with tears as she hurried out. Since the meal had now reached the final stages, she excused herself and followed the girl, to find her weeping against the wall outside.

Anna touched her shoulder gently. The girl jerked round, looking terrified, and stammered an apology.

"You must not cry. My cousin is not so very angry with you. You are new, aren't you?"

"Yes, *citoyenne*," stammered the girl.

"What is your name?"

"Jeanne," said the girl with a curtsy.

"Well, Jeanne, dry your eyes. There, that is better. Do you come from Paris?"

Gradually, with a soothing voice, she drew from the girl that she was lately arrived from the country and very homesick. Plump, rosy-faced, Jeanne was at sea in the city, which seemed to her enormous and frightening.

"Have you no friends or relatives in Paris?" asked Anna, touched by the girl's child-like manner.

"My brother Jacques," said Jeanne, her face lighting up. "He keeps a shop in the Faubourg Saint-Antoine. *Mère* Conjou has said I may visit him one day."

"Will that make you feel more at home?" asked Anna, and the girl's bright eyes were answer enough.

Anna went down to see *Mère* Conjou, the lodging-house keeper, who was, as always, seated in her dark little room by the entrance polishing her silver. She gave Anna a frog-like glare from her small eyes, sniffing.

"Jeanne? She has been here two days. She is not entitled to any time off."

"Citizen Feuvielle sent my uncle three dozen larks last week, but we had only two dozen in the pie," said Anna. "And the brace of ducks Leslin sent us from Versailles disappeared without trace." She smiled blandly at *Mère* Conjou, who stiffened.

Her small, stiff little fingers paused in their rubbing motion. She looked at Anna sharply, then stretched her mouth in a frigid smile.

"Of course, *citoyenne*, if you interest yourself in the girl I shall see what can be done. Tomorrow morning I have to send to the Faubourg Saint-Antoine for some new baize, and Jeanne may perform this errand for me."

Anna returned the smile. "You are very kind, *citoyenne*. Thank you."

She knew that it was expected that certain household items might be discreetly sold by the housekeeper, but *Mère* Conjou went beyond the pale with her pilferings, and Anna had intended to speak to her uncle about a change in their lodgings. The lodgings were comfortable, it was true, and a move might be disastrous, but she felt it would do no harm to let *Mère* Conjou know that she suspected her.

Jeanne was hovering in the passage as she emerged, and gave a sigh of radiant disbelief when Anna told her the news.

"You are too good, *citoyenne!*" Seizing Anna's hand, she kissed it before running away.

Anna turned, very flushed, and bumped into their dinner guest, Yves Saint-Denis, who smiled at her pleasantly.

"Ah, there you are, *citoyenne.* I was looking for you to thank you. I must leave now as I have some business to perform, but I wished to say how much I enjoyed the evening."

"I am sorry you must go," she said, absently. "Perhaps you could come back later? We have many guests in the salon tonight."

He shook his head. "Alas, I should be delighted, but it will be impossible. Another day, perhaps?"

She looked up at him, seeing him clearly for the first time. She had been too absorbed during dinner to take much notice of him, particularly since her uncle's friends tended to be cut from the same cloth, didactic, dogmatic, argumentative and politically obsessed.

She could not remember having met Yves Saint-Denis before, although the name was familiar to her from her uncle's conversation. Had she done so, in any case, she was not sure she would remember, as this man was not someone to make an instant impression.

Big, very broad in the shoulder, with brown hair cut simply *en brosse,* he had clear gray eyes which saw a good deal, and a pleasant open face. His expression of frank good humor was, she suspected, deceptive. There was intelligence and reserve behind the smile, shrewdness and wit in the gray eyes.

Now he raised his brows inquiringly. "I am glad we have met at last, *citoyenne,*" he said in a soft voice.

She flushed, realizing she had been staring at him. "At last?" she queried.

"I have seen you often, but we have never been introduced," he told her.

Her blank gaze admitted that she had no recollection of having seen him before, and he smiled again.

"I hope that next time we shall have more time in which to improve our acquaintance."

He lifted her hand in a courtly gesture which had not been seen in Paris for a long time, kissed her hand lightly, bowed, and was gone.

When Anna joined the others in the salon she found that another guest had arrived.

He was bending over Maria's chair, but as Anna entered he looked up and gave her a wickedly amused grin on catching the expression of distance she could not suppress.

Anna flushed and looked away. There was something about this man Feuvielle that alarmed her.

Tall, very lean, with dark brown hair turning silver at the temples, he was in his late thirties. His dark eyes twinkled with comprehension; he was, indeed, in her opinion, altogether too acute. His long mouth curved sensually, marked at the corners with lines of experience, cynicism and humor.

He was dangerously attractive.

Rumor had it that he had been a notorious rake in the high days of the French court. He had spent his youth in a succession of wild love affairs, duels and gambling. And then he had astonished everyone by renouncing his title and becoming one of the intellectual leaders of the radical party. He was now detested and despised by his own class, but his voice was heard in the most influential quarters.

Anna did not like to see him so intimate with Maria. She was relieved when her uncle began to talk to him about the latest news. All Parisians read the newspapers with nervous intensity since the revolution. Each day was fraught with danger. Feuvielle listened to Sir Henry, a satanic droop to his eyelids.

"I have just come from a meeting," he said now, leaning back in his chair casually. "They are planning to arrest all British citizens very soon. You would be wise to leave France at once."

Sir Henry's eyes blinked rapidly, as they always did under stress, but he jerked up his chin. "It will blow over. They have threatened it before."

"This time they mean it," Feuvielle insisted. "After all, France is at war with England."

"It is the Austrians who threaten them," Sir Henry said with a familiar, stubborn ring to his voice.

"The nation all France fears is England, my friend," Feuvielle said. "And you are English."

Sir Henry reddened, his eyes bulging. "I am not! I am a Scot!"

Feuvielle laughed.

Sir Henry bristled, eyeing him angrily. "And I think I am well known as a Friend of the Revolution."

"There are hundreds of British citizens in France," Feuvielle drawled. "Do you think they will sort you out like a housewife sorting the best apples? No, they will tumble you all into prison without discrimination."

"I have friends!"

Feuvielle's shrug was tolerant. "Oh, yes, we are all your friends, my dear Sir Henry. But I doubt we could do much for you. The people are very hostile to England at present. You would be wiser to leave France now."

Sir Henry snorted fearsomely, his gaze scornful of the other man's advice.

Feuvielle eyed him with wry amusement. After a little pause he said softly: "I would hate to see Miss Anna and Miss Maria thrust into prison, my friend."

Sir Henry's lips quivered more rapidly than ever. He stared across the salon at Maria, who had not listened to a word of the discussion, and was busy twining one of her golden ringlets around her finger to give it more curl.

"My daughter?" he whispered hoarsely. "Good God, it never entered my head that they would harm her!" He stared anxiously at Feuvielle. "They would not arrest young girls, man?"

The Frenchman's dark eyes glowed cynically. "And children, too, my dear Sir Henry. Babes in arms are being taken." The drawled retort was charged with irony. "You English are so naïve! A revolution is not accomplished by kindness. Decision is necessary. The stakes are our very lives. Men with so much to lose are cruel if they feel they have to be so."

Sir Henry's voice shook. "Maria . . . my helpless, delicate child. God forgive me—what danger have I plunged her into?"

Anna, listening intently, met Feuvielle's eyes and was amazed to find his satanic brows lifted in wicked, intimate fashion, as though they shared a joke. She gave him a frosty glance and looked away. He need not expect her to laugh because her uncle was blind to the tough, self-protective quality which Maria masked with sweet smiles and demure little ways.

If it made Sir Henry happy to believe her a helpless, innocent child, then Anna was ready to pretend to agree. He had suffered enough disillusionment over the revolution. A personal disillusionment would wound him unbearably.

Another of their guests arrived at that moment, and Sir Henry broke off the conversation to greet him. One by one they came into the salon, mainly men involved in politics, their conversation on the one absorbing topic.

There was Scarret, small, busy and self-important, his pockets stuffed with papers, his shirt spotted by soup stains. And René Lagrett, tall, cadaverous and capable of wild bursts of manic laughter on the most surprising occasions. Jean Poulet came in talking angrily of the scarcity of bread, the restlessness of the people and the dropping value of the new money.

"The assignat's lost value again today," he complained, his beaky nose quivering. "The Committee must do something, Feuvielle. It must act now!"

"We are doing all we can," Feuvielle said curtly. "The drought has reduced the flow of grain by two-thirds. We are not magicians. We cannot conjure it out of thin air."

René burst out into one of his shrieks of laughter, and then explained that he had seen something funny on his way there. "A woman dropped a crust of bread and before she could pick it up a dozen brats had fallen upon it. She was knocked over in the gutter and got up covered in filth, cursing and screaming like a madwoman!" His bulging eyes seethed with wild amusement as he spoke, and Anna shivered.

The picture terrified and moved her. Poor woman, she thought, remembering the excellent meal she had just eaten. She had never known what it was to go hungry. She looked around the elegant salon. Their guests lounged in brocade-covered chairs, nibbling and sipping wine. The poor could not indulge in macaroons. They could not even buy bread. When one remembered that, one felt a heavy load settle on the heart. Outside, in the dark and narrow streets, men and women were going hungry to bed, their minds filled with bitterness. And the children, dirty, ragged little creatures who had never eaten meat in their lives, no doubt, sleeping curled on a cold floor with empty stomachs.

She looked at René Lagrett with anger, but noticed suddenly that beneath his wild laughter burned a fierce rage that such things should happen, and her own anger died.

Across the room sat Feuvielle, playing with Maria's pretty fan. Anna's eyes met his and she was astonished to find sympathy in his face, as though he had read her thoughts. Was that why he had taken up the revolutionary cause? Did he, too, feel angry that children should go hungry?

Feuvielle stood up to hand Maria back her fan. She saw his dark face mobile and outrageous, heard his voice speaking quickly, with vivid gestures. Maria's blue eyes gleamed in amusement. The expression on her small face hit Anna like a blow across the cheek. Surely, she thought with shocked amazement, surely Maria is not in love with him? Good God, no!

Someone was standing beside her. She heard a harsh intake of breath. Looking round she recognized Louis Baccoult.

"Good evening," she smiled politely. Had he, too, been watching Maria and Feuvielle? Had he noticed that revealing look on Maria's enchanting face?

He was very pale, his eyes miserable. *"Citoyenne,"* he began in a hurried whisper, "I beg you to warn your cousin against Feuvielle. He is without scruple where women are concerned . . ."

"Please!" she interrupted, flushing. "I cannot discuss such things with you! If my uncle dislikes the acquaintance he will speak to my cousin."

He trembled, wringing his hands together. "He may not know the truth about him."

"My cousin is not foolish, citizen," she said gently. "She would do nothing against her conscience." It was, after all, one way of describing Maria's levelheaded selfishness. And it was true that Maria never made indiscretions, since she never lost her head.

"She is so innocent," he protested.

Anna smiled at him. Poor boy, she thought, it is you who are the innocent!

"What are you about, Louis? Flirting with Anna? I had not thought you were so cruel!" Maria glided up to them, blue eyes reproachful, and Louis gazed at her in bewildered delight. She took his hand and led him away, giving Anna a sharp look over her shoulder as she went.

Feuvielle joined Anna and grinned lazily at her. "You have too tender a heart, *citoyenne*," he drawled.

She gave him a cool look and turned to go, but he caught her arm. She looked meaningfully at his thin fingers clasped about her wrist.

"Sir!"

He laughed softly. "You are concerned for young Baccoult. You need not be. Young pups must learn that pretty kittens have sharp claws."

"Must he be scarred in the process?" she asked, then bit her lip, wishing she could recall the words. It would have been more modest to pretend ignorance of his meaning.

His dark eyes danced. "Ah, as I had long suspected! You are sharp-tongued as well as sharp-eyed." He steered her into a corner and pulled up a small gilt chair. "The young learn only by experience, my dear Miss. He must be badly scratched before he will realize what manner of creature he has been pursuing."

Anna was not to be lured into further indiscretion. She set her chin at a determined angle and said politely: "Do you think this hot weather will last, citizen?"

He laughed loudly, drawing curious stares upon them, and on the other side of the room Maria, looking up, scowled to see them sitting so snugly together, and, losing her temper, spoke with spiteful asperity to Louis Baccoult.

"Marry you?" she laughed crossly. "It is insulting even to suggest it! A penniless law student with no prospects and no family worth mentioning! I hope I have more common sense than to throw myself away like that. Marry you, indeed!" Her laughter was cruel and incisive. "Why, you are impudent, sir, as well as boring."

He was stunned into immobility, his color draining totally away as he stared into the enchanting face, now filled with spite and vicious temper. Even Maria noticed how white he had become, and irritably hoped he would not disgrace her by fainting.

She got up, her fan flickering like a butterfly, and walked hurriedly away.

Anna, watching them, saw Louis gaze after her with eyes that looked like great black pools of misery. Then the boy walked quickly out of the salon, his head sunk on his chest.

Feuvielle whistled softly under his breath. "So!"

Maria joined them, smiling brightly, but her blue

eyes stabbing at her cousin from behind the pretty fan.

"Every time I see you, dear Anna," she cooed, "you are flirting with one of *my* beaux!" Her cheeks were imprinted with bright red coins of temper.

Feuvielle lifted one of the tiny white hands and kissed it with graceful emphasis. "You look very cross, my pretty. I suspect you are jealous."

She tossed her head. "Jealous? I?" She laughed crossly. "What nonsense! I am sure I do not need to be jealous of Anna." And the blue eyes dismissed her cousin with contempt.

On the following morning, Maria went shopping with her maid, to buy ribbons with which to decorate her new bonnet. Anna took the opportunity of tidying her cousin's room, sighing as she considered the tangled contents of Maria's chest of drawers. This task should have been performed by the maid, but Anna knew that she would wait until eternity before it was done, and to complain to Maria would only mean a scene and, possibly, the departure of the maid, with all the inconvenience which that would entail. It was easier and more pleasant to do it oneself.

Maria had graciously given Anna a gown she had grown tired of, a blue silk ball gown, with a full train in darker velvet, which had been a little too long for Maria but would just fit her cousin.

"You are such a beanpole," Maria said idly, "I keep tripping over the hem, but it will fit you well enough, I dare say."

When Anna had reduced the turmoil to manageable proportions, she tried on the blue silk, and found it fitted her to perfection.

The neckline was a trifle low. She preferred a more modest style, but she had to admit, gazing at herself in the mirror, that it suited her.

Her thick chestnut hair hung down over her shoulders, brushed until it shone, curling down into the whiteness of her bosom. The blue silk shimmered as she moved, throwing up the color of her eyes.

Why, she thought, blushing, I look quite pretty. She had never possessed so adult a gown before, since Maria always chose her gowns, claiming to have more idea of taste, and Maria's idea of a suitable gown for Anna was always unassuming. Muslins and plain day wear, as for a very young girl, made up the bulk of Anna's wardrobe. Maria intended to have no rivals. Considering her own reflection, Anna could not repress an amused suspicion that Maria would regret her gift when she saw how it suited the recipient.

A tap on the door made her jump.

"Entrez," she called, and one of the other maids, a slatternly girl with a permanent cold, pushed her head into the room. Anna, half expecting Jeanne, looked disappointed, but smiled.

"Citoyenne, c'est Citoyen Baccoult," the maid mumbled, staring curiously at Anna, in her unaccustomed finery.

Anna sighed. Louis, she thought! Poor boy. She wondered what he wanted. Reluctantly, she went down to the salon, and opened the door.

In the middle of the room stood a tall, broad-shouldered man whom she did not recognize. He was staring about him, hands on hips, his profile towards her.

The silly girl confused the name, Anna decided.

Then, hearing the rustle of her silk gown, the stranger spun on his heels, and a pair of furious black eyes met hers.

She blinked at the ferocity of that gaze. Wild black hair fell in curls to his ears, his face was lean, tough, marked with bitterness and impatience.

His eyes flickered over her in a manner she found decidedly insolent. She was angry to feel herself blushing.

Then he spoke, in a swift Parisian accent which she found difficult to follow.

"So! I wondered what you would look like!" He advanced, lip curling, and stood close to her, staring with those angry eyes. "Louis is very young, but I had not expected him to be taken in by society manners and fine clothes! He has been a fool, and he is well paid for his folly!"

Clearly, he mistook her for Maria, and she began to explain his error, but he cut her stammering short with one curt gesture.

"Oh, do not play off your tricks on me, *citoyenne!* I am not an impressionable boy. I am proof against your pretty ways."

"Who are you?" Anna demanded, growing angry herself.

"Charles Baccoult," he snapped, "Louis's brother."

She looked up at him in startled interest. Yes, she saw, there was a resemblance. Louis had a smoother, less experienced face. But this man had all of his brother's handsome looks, although they were marred by the passage of years and the bitterness of his temper.

He was watching her in his turn, sneering slightly. "You comprehend why I am here, I see. Your face reveals your guilt."

"My what?" Her voice rose in amazement. She searched his face with wide blue eyes, uneasy as the memory of Louis's face filled her head.

"I came because I wanted to see the girl who had destroyed my brother," he went on harshly.

Anna felt the blood leave her cheeks. She moved

backward, fumbling for a chair, and sank down on the edge of the seat. Her eyes could not look away from his dark, intent face. A feeling of shock and horror swept over her as she waited, unable to speak herself, and dreading his next words.

Two

"I see," he sneered, "that you are quick-witted, *citoyenne*. Or were you expecting something of the sort? Perhaps you are like the savages of America and only feel your power when you have scalps dangling from your belt?"

She shook her head confusedly. "What has happened to Louis?" she demanded in a voice that shook.

The black eyes narrowed. "He tried to kill himself." His words were abrupt and cold. He studied their effect upon her with a frown.

Wincing, she clasped her hands together in her lap, her head bent. Then she looked up, realizing what he had said. "Tried?" she asked breathlessly.

He shrugged. "He took poison. By chance, I arrived early at the house, and found him alive but unconscious. I am a doctor. I knew what to do. I worked on him all night. He is out of danger now."

"Thank God," she whispered, closing her eyes in relief. Oh, she thought, I should have followed Louis last night, attempted to comfort him. Had he died I would have been partly responsible. I knew what a

blow he had suffered. I saw the misery in his face.
Yet I let him go without a word. Poor boy, how he
must have felt to do this thing!

"Hypocrite!" Charles Baccoult snarled, lips drawn
back from his teeth in contempt. "Do you think to
deceive me with this charade of sorrow? Louis told
me everything! He sees you as you are now, *citoyenne*. You encouraged him to love you, for a mere
whim! Flirted with him, threw him smiles, as you
might throw a bone to a dog. But Louis was no lap-
dog, was he? He dared to ask you to marry him.
And then he felt the full force of your true nature.
Then you tore off the fashionable mask and let him
see the coldhearted whore beneath!"

"Oh!" Anna shrank back, appalled by his violence.
She stood up hastily and tried to push past him, but
he caught her by the shoulders, shaking her.

"No, *citoyenne*. You shall listen. It is time you
heard the truth about that shriveled walnut you call
your heart!"

She looked up, eyes huge, and saw herself reflected
in his eyes, minute and shining. His dark face seemed
to swim down at her, taut, filled with savagery.

"Louis was too far beneath you to be considered
as a husband, was he not?" he asked scornfully. "He
was amusing in your drawing-room, adoring you on
his knees. But when he stood up and asked you to be
his wife . . . his equal . . . then, ah, then, *citoyenne*,
you felt insulted. You used the full savagery of your
tongue on him, and sent him running home in
despair."

Anna listened, unable to stop the flow, her temples
pounding, her pulses beating like drums. He was, she
felt, beyond hearing her. His anger consumed him.

At last, he drew breath, still holding her, and
closed his eyes momentarily in a look of weariness.

"*Citoyen*," Anna ventured, in a shaking voice,

"you have made a mistake. I am not Maria Campbell."

The lids slowly rose from his eyes. He looked down, his brows drawing together above the strong nose.

"What?" he demanded tersely.

"You asked for *Citoyenne* Campbell," she whispered, quivering at the menace of his gaze. "There are two of us—I am Anna Campbell, Maria's cousin. The maid made a mistake."

He stared at her, from head to foot, then a dark red tide rose in his face.

"You allowed me to make such a fool of myself," he ground out angrily. "Why the devil didn't you tell me?"

"You would not let me speak," she whispered.

His eyes flashed. "God in heaven!" He shook her violently, his face contorted.

"Mon Dieu, what is happening here?"

Charles Baccoult released her and Anna slumped back into her chair, breathing hard. She heard the salon door close quietly and footsteps cross towards them, but she did not look up.

"Out of my way," snarled Charles Baccoult.

"Why, no! *Citoyen,* I think you should explain before you go!" The new voice was calm, quiet, yet threaded with determination. She recognized it.

"It is a private matter. None of your damned business."

"Violence is never private, *citoyen.* One does not use such brutality to a female."

Charles Baccoult laughed, savagely. "Fool!"

There was the sound of a scuffle, the crack of bone on bone, and a thud.

The door slammed and Anna ran to where a gentleman sprawled on the floor. As she knelt beside him he sat up, rubbing his jaw ruefully.

The expression on his pleasant face brought a bubble of slightly hysterical laughter into her throat. An answering smile came into his gray eyes.

"I am glad to see that you are not harmed, *citoyenne*," he murmured, rising to his feet and assisting her with a gentle hand. She became aware of the embarrassment of her position, and flushed.

What must he think? She stared at the floor, trying to think of something to say.

"I do not wish to pry, *citoyenne*, but your visitor seemed a dangerous fellow. You should inform your uncle of this incident. He will know how to deal with it."

She looked up in alarm. "Oh, no! Please, do not mention it to my uncle!"

He looked sharply at her, frowning. "It is not, of course, my business, but do you think it wise to conceal the matter? He was a handsome fellow, and you are very young. Allow me to intrude some well-meant advice . . ."

She laughed nervously. "Please, *Citoyen* Saint-Denis, I assure you, I am not in love with him. You mistake me."

Yves Saint-Denis rubbed his jaw again. "I am concerned, nevertheless, *citoyenne*. Could you not confide in me? We lawyers are discreet fellows, you know." His smile reassured her.

"The situation is complicated," she murmured. "He mistook me for someone else. I cannot confide in my uncle without breaking faith with . . ." she could say no more without endangering Maria, and stopped short, biting her lip.

As she had suspected on their first meeting, Yves Saint-Denis was quick-witted and shrewd. He watched her, frowning for a moment. Then, "He mistook you for Miss Maria?"

Anna was thrown into nervous confusion. "I

should not have said so much! Please, do not repeat what I have said!"

"Of course I shall not, if you desire it," he said, still frowning. "But if your cousin puts you at such risks . . ."

"She does not know what has occurred," she said quickly. "And I informed him of his mistake, so that it is not likely to happen again. He was angry. But I think he will not come back."

He gestured in resignation. "You must admit, the situation must arouse curiosity. And concern."

"Please, forget what happened," she said. "I cannot explain further. It was too personal a matter to discuss with a stranger."

He bowed. "I understand. But if ever you need a discreet friend I will be willing to do whatever I can for you. I do not want you to have to face such a business again."

She was startled and grateful. "You are very kind."

"It would be a great pleasure to serve you, *citoyenne*," he murmured.

She flushed and hurriedly offered him refreshments, ringing the bell.

"You are very kind," he accepted, seating himself with a flick of his coat-tails. "Coffee is always most welcome. I have been talking all the morning and my throat is parched. If there is one thing I dislike in my profession it is the amount of talking I have to do. Listening I find pleasant, thank God."

She moved to the side table and found a small bowl of sweet meats which were kept there. She offered them to him and he smilingly took one.

"I have a sweet tooth," he confessed, with his charming smile.

As she returned the bowl to its place she caught sight of herself in the mirror which hung on the salon wall. A face white with remembered terror gazed back, eyes like blue smudges, under drawn brows, lips tinged with little spots of blood where she had bitten them.

The man was a barbarian, she thought. Accustomed to the calm civilities of salon life, she was still dazed by the violence with which he had accused her.

"Has your uncle heard the rumors coming out from the Committee of Public Safety?" Yves asked her, making her jump. "They are said to be planning the arrest of all British citizens. I hope it is all idle gossip."

A moment later Sir Henry himself arrived, welcoming his friend with a smile, and Anna quietly slipped away to her own room.

That evening, she spoke to Jeanne about her visit to her brother in the Faubourg Saint-Antoine. The girl chattered excitedly, still elated by her reunion with her brother. He kept a wine shop in the Rue des Arbres, she told Anna. There were no trees there, though, she admitted, her expression naïvely crestfallen. That was strange, was it not, *citoyenne?* And the houses were so close together! But her brother had been very kind. They had drunk a bottle of their home-grown wine, and talked of the old days, and their family.

"Jacques says one day we will set up in a lodging house of our own. When I am trained in service. Jacques means to marry a girl from our old home. I shall see to the housekeeping. Jacques will attend to the wine and the accounts, and his wife will be the cook." She sighed dreamily. "He will make sure he marries a good cook, of course. That is essential."

"You have it all planned!" Anna laughed.

Jeanne blushed. "Jacques says it is necessary to know what one wants of the world," she stammered.

"I am sure he is right," Anna nodded, seeing that her amusement had stung the girl. She looked at her gently. Fifteen, cheerful, eager to learn, she was a likable and pleasing child. "I will teach you as much as I can, Jeanne," she offered.

Jeanne thanked her with delight.

"I must go now," Anna said. "I do not want my uncle to be cross with me."

Jeanne giggled. *"Citoyen* Campbell is often cross," she said. "But not for long, I think! He is too kind."

Anna laughed back, touched by this view of her uncle. It was a very clear-sighted summing up of his character, she thought, as she joined him in the salon.

Yves was dining with them. His presence made the meal more pleasant than usual. Maria, having assessed his potential, ignored him with a toss of her curls. She would not waste ammunition on a man whose gray eyes met hers with cool indifference, especially as he was, to her mind, a dull old lawyer.

Afterwards they were joined by Feuvielle, casually elegant as always, who devoted himself to Maria, while Yves sat beside Anna and talked of books, music and poetry. She found him extraordinarily easy to talk to and fell naturally into talk of England, after touching upon the subject of English poetry.

It was so long ago that she had left Kent to live in London with Sir Henry that her memories had blurred into a dim and misty beauty. Silver rain slanting down on rolling green meadows. Elms and oaks shading grazing sheep. The gleam of white chalk through grass. The long dark shadow passing over the downs as the sun moved across the sky.

She talked on and on, in irregular sentences, her voice betraying her deep homesickness, surprised to realize herself how deeply she felt.

He watched her expressive, mobile face, smiling. "You long for home," he suggested.

She blushed and faltered into silence, suddenly

aware of how revealing her eagerness must be, and nodded.

"I, too," he said. His own countryside was not gently rolling like hers, he said, but lay at the foot of mountains. White mists rose to reveal white peaks high above the land. Wild birds swept down on autumn winds, winds which took the lungs by surprise and left one gasping but exultant.

"I hate to live in the town," he grimaced, "but my profession demands it!"

He was so different to the excitable Parisians she was accustomed to meet. His slow, calm temperament reminded her of the Kent yeomen whom she had known so well as a child.

Yves had, however, as deep a faith in the revolution as any Parisian. Like most of the professional middle class, he had long resented the aristocracy who blocked his path. Listening to his calm voice, she felt that he was far more impressive than the more volatile and explosive Parisians. His very calmness made him dangerous to those who opposed him.

She suddenly became aware that Feuvielle and her uncle were talking excitedly on the far side of the room. Maria sat clutching her little pet dog, Frou, well aware that this formed a pleasing picture.

"My dear," Sir Henry said to his daughter, "Feuvielle thinks I should send you two girls out of the country."

Maria stiffened and shot Feuvielle a glance from narrowed eyes. She was piqued at the idea that he could contemplate with apparent indifference the notion of her departure from Paris.

"Go home to England?" she asked, beginning to pout. From beneath lowered lids her acquisitive little eyes studied Feuvielle. How handsome he was, she thought, and how maddeningly enigmatic. What was he thinking, his dark eyes humorously fixed on her?

With a quirk of his satanic brows, Feuvielle explained, "It would be difficult to get to England. The Channel ports are watched. But I am going to Switzerland tomorrow on official business, and I will not be questioned as to any ladies in my entourage." His wicked smile challenged Maria, whose pink mouth curled in understanding.

Anna stared, a startled exclamation on her lips. Surely Uncle Henry would not permit this? Across the salon her eyes met those of Feuvielle. He grinned quizzically.

Maria's glance followed his and her lips tightened. She did not like the way Anna was always flirting with Feuvielle, she decided. Might it account for his elusive attitude to herself? One day she was convinced she had him in the hollow of her hand. The next he had slipped away, smiling, mocking, impossible to pin down. Could it be possible that Anna attracted him?

Aloud she said, "Anna must go, of course, Papa, but I could not leave you alone in Paris. One of us must stay with you." She moved to him, eyes misty, her little heart-shaped face full of brave determination. "I will not desert you, Papa."

Feuvielle watched with cynical appreciation, eyes dancing. Maria, giving him a sidelong peep, was infuriated by the blatant mockery of his expression.

Sir Henry patted her cheek, coughing to hide his emotion. "My dearest child, how could I bear it if anything happened to you! You must go."

She bit her lip, fluttering her thick lashes. "Oh, what shall I do?" She threw Anna a glance of wistful appeal. "Someone must look after you, Papa!" She leaned her cheek against him. "I will try to do all that Anna does to make you comfortable, although I know I am not so clever and capable as she is . . ." A deep sigh. "How I wish I were more like Anna!"

"I shall be very happy to stay," Anna said calmly. She felt foolish, drawn into this emotional scene before two strangers. Why could not Maria have waited to stage her little drama? Anna had had no intention of leaving her uncle alone in Paris, or of traveling to Switzerland with Feuvielle. But she would have preferred to discuss it *en famille*.

Sir Henry protested. Anna reassured him. Maria wept and secretly brooded over Feuvielle's amused grin. One day, she thought dreamily, I will have him at my mercy—and then let him feel like laughing at me!

Yves gently warned Sir Henry that he should leave France himself. "Matters are coming to a head," he said grimly. "The Girondins are finished. Something very unpleasant is growing in Paris."

Troubled, uneasy, yet stubborn, Sir Henry said he would finish his business arrangements before leaving. There was no immediate danger.

Yves and Feuvielle exchanged wry glances, shrugging. Yves glanced at Anna, his brow troubled.

"This is madness," he murmured in a low voice. "Go with your cousin! Your uncle is not a child."

She smiled, shaking her head. "Oh, but he is," she said. "You have no idea! If I were not here, he would forget to change his clothes, or catch cold from sheer absent-mindedness."

"Your cousin, I think, did not wish you to go," he said in a critical voice, looking at Maria with cold eyes.

Anna sighed. "Yes, that does cause me anxiety. My uncle does not see that she desired to be alone with Feuvielle. I hope she knows what she is doing."

"His reputation is doubtful," he whispered, "yet I have always found him trustworthy. He is a cynic, certainly."

Anna sighed again. "Celeste will travel with Maria, of course, Uncle," she said aloud.

Maria looked smug. Celeste, being French, expected her English mistress to be indiscreet. She would be easy to manage.

Feuveille grinned at Anna. "My sister will chaperone Miss Maria," he drawled wickedly.

"Your sister?" Maria's voice rose shrilly, and red color blossomed in her cheeks.

Feuvielle bowed, eyes sardonic. "She accompanies me, *citoyenne*. I would not otherwise have suggested this plan. Nor, I am sure, would your father have consented."

With this he withdrew, Sir Henry following him. Yves made his own *adieux* and hurriedly withdrew, not wishing to be present when Maria's obvious rage burst forth.

"Have you met his sister?" Maria screamed, her face now pale puce. "She has a face like a gargoyle, and wears gowns of acid green or black, and bonnets so festooned with feathers that it is like walking with a parrot. And her conversation! La! I declare she is the most dull, unendurably stupid female I have ever met!"

"Hush," said Anna, fearing this would reach the ears of the gentlemen, whose voices could be heard departing.

"Oh, how dared he!" Maria stamped her foot, screwing up her mouth as though tasting a lemon. "He knew very well what I would reply to a suggestion of traveling to Switzerland with her!"

Vainly Anna pointed out that it would be interesting to visit Switzerland.

"Snow and clocks!" retorted Maria furiously. "And endless cow bells!"

"Lake Geneva is reckoned very beautiful," offered Anna.

But Maria did not hear, her little hands curled into claws. "Oh, I could pull every hair from his head!" she hissed.

Her rage increased when Sir Henry informed her that she would be staying in Geneva with his old friend, the banker Gregory MacAndrew, and his charming family. Two pretty little girls for Maria to talk to, he said happily. Maria looked explosively at Anna, who hurriedly guided her out of the room.

Early next morning, as Anna packed for her, Maria kicked a bonnet into a corner, her lovely face discontented. "MacAndrew! Two little girls to play with! Why, I might as well enter a convent. I thought I might have some fun on this journey, but it seems I am due to be bored to death. First Feuvielle's dragon of a sister. Now a straitlaced Presbyterian family who will probably keep me in a cupboard as though I were made of china!"

"I am relieved that you will be in such good hands," said Anna unsympathetically, picking up the bonnet and attempting to straighten its bent feathers.

Maria giggled, looking slyly at her. "Oh, well, I may have a chance to flirt with Feuvielle when we stop at inns en route. His sister cannot be with me all the time."

"Feuvielle is dangerous, Maria," said Anna in alarm.

"That is what I like in him," admitted Maria shamelessly. "Flirting with him is like going into a tiger's cage! You must admire him, Anna. How can one not? That graceful, menacing walk! Those glowing eyes! He is an exciting animal." Her pink lips parted moistly, eyes shining. "One wonders what it would be like . . ." she paused, giving Anna a secret look.

"Tigers," said Anna flatly, forcing down her anxiety, "have a habit of devouring their prey."

Maria giggled. She loved to walk near the edge of the cliff, playing with danger. "He is a mysterious creature," she murmured. "A cynic with a past . . ."

Anna looked disgusted. "Why will you read those silly Gothic novels, Maria?"

"Oh, do not be so prosy," Maria snapped.

"It was not at all exciting to have Louis's brother accusing me of breaking the boy's heart," Anna said flatly. She looked directly at her cousin. "How would your Gothic novels handle that?"

Maria looked peevish. "I have said I am sorry you were so frightened. The man must be mad, coming here like that! Is it my fault Louis was so weak-spirited?" She ran one small hand over her face, thoughtfully. It was rather flattering, after all, she decided, to have a man kill himself for love of you. And Louis had been very handsome. But he could not compare with Feuvielle. What was youth to experience, after all?

Anna sighed. What use to discuss it with her? "Do you want this bonnet now?" she asked, holding it up, the bent feathers drooping. "It was new last week. Why could you not kick one of your older ones?"

Maria giggled, then looked at it with regret. It was a pretty thing, she thought. "If you bought some new trimmings, Anna, you would just have time to mend it before I leave! I think I would prefer a darker feather this time. Just run down and buy one, will you?"

Anna felt like stamping on the bonnet, but she controlled her temper. Maria walked down with her to the front door, giving her a list of other small items she wanted. As they stood on the steps, Maria listening with a pout to Anna's refusal to search out the exact shade of pink to match her petticoat ribbons, Anna stiffened and without a word pushed her back into the hall, closing the door with a slam.

"Anna, have you run mad?" demanded Maria, furious.

"He was out there," babbled Anna, beginning to tremble, and eyeing the door as though it might explode at any moment.

"Who?" Maria looked baffled.

"Charles Baccoult," stammered Anna. "And, oh, Maria! If you had seen his face! He is coming here again—to see you this time!"

Three

Maria shrieked. "I must hide!" She, too, stared in horror at the closed door, as though expecting Charles Baccoult to force his way inside at any moment.

"Go to your room," Anna ordered, still shaking, but growing calmer as she reviewed the situation. There were, after all, servants within call, and Sir Henry and Feuvielle would be here soon.

Maria, instead, went to the salon and peered out of the window at the street, keeping herself out of sight.

"Come here, Anna—which is he?" Her eyes darted up and down, inspecting the passers-by with curiosity.

Anna joined her nervously. "There," she said, pointing. "Oh, he is walking away! He has changed his mind!"

"That one? I can only see his back. What a pity! I would have liked to see him closer."

Anna, exhausted by her little panic of fear, gave her cousin a disgusted glance. Maria seemed merely curious and excited. She had not been faced with Charles Baccoult yet.

As they looked out, Sir Henry and Feuvielle arrived in the carriage, piled high with luggage, and Maria gave a cry of consternation. "It is too late now to furnish up my bonnet! Oh, how annoying! Never mind, Anna. You can keep it. I shall not want it, I dare say. And you can have all my other things. I left so many ribbons and petticoats behind . . ."

Sir Henry was deeply affected by this parting, and had to keep so stern a hold upon his emotions that he seemed almost cold as he kissed his daughter good-bye.

Anna watched him anxiously, seeing the hard shine of his eyes. She could gladly have smacked Maria for the gay indifference of her farewell. The other girl was far too excited by her coming adventure to pretend any deep grief. It would not have hurt her, thought Anna grimly, to have summoned up some of the tears she shed so easily on other occasions.

Feuvielle kissed Anna's hand, flickering an intimate, sardonic glance at her. "She will be safe with me!" he whispered.

She met his glance directly. "I hope so!"

His lips twitched. "Such a dutiful cousin," he murmured.

Maria was watching them suspiciously, and came forward, her small hand closing possessively around Feuvielle's sleeve.

Anna stood on the steps, waving her handkerchief, until the carriage had vanished. Sir Henry muttered something about urgent business, and vanished too, leaving Anna to clear up the turmoil left in Maria's chamber. Gowns, ribbons, lace lay sprawled everywhere, and she was some time about the task.

Her mind was occupied with questions about

Charles Baccoult. Why had he gone away? She had
been so certain that he intended to come to the
house. Their eyes had met briefly before she hurried
back inside. She had seen the hard, cruel twist of his
mouth. The bitter face had been intent upon Maria
at first, then moved to her with a little grimace. Why
had he changed his mind?

Jeanne sidled in nervously with a cup of hot
chocolate, still rather lacking confidence but hoping
to be welcomed, like a little puppy who fears rejec-
tion. Anna, pushing away the dangerous image of
Charles Baccoult, smiled at her. "Are you beginning
to enjoy living in Paris yet?"

"Oh, yes, *citoyenne*," returned Jeanne eagerly, and
her busy little tongue launched into a description of
a brief visit to the Champs Elysées on an errand for
Mère Conjou.

Anna had often been amazed by the way in which
the normal, happy life of the city continued during
these dark days, almost as the stylized backcloth to a
ferocious tragedy, with people crowding the shops,
the theaters, the restaurants; promenading in their
best clothes down the Champs Elysées, watching
puppet shows with their children, or buying refreshments at little booths set up alongside, where singers
trilled artistically, or fiddlers played for the young
people to dance.

Not here, of course, did one find the poorest citizens. They had no money for pleasure. All their
energies were needed to keep themselves alive.

Anna, for all her sympathy towards the revolution,
had not been able to forget the September Massacres,
in which hundreds of innocent men, women and
children had been brutally and viciously hacked to
death by men whispered to have been especially
brought to Paris from the prisons of Marseilles.
People dared not openly discuss why and how this

evil had been perpetrated, but rumor, like autumn fog, crept slowly through the city.

Those responsible were now in command of the revolution. Cold, calculating, ruthless men. Anna shivered, listening to Jeanne's chattering. She hoped her uncle would soon be ready to leave France. Every day brought them nearer disaster.

She bent over the pile of discarded clothes on the bed and found a pair of red-heeled shoes. They were a little scuffed, the silk had lost its first sheen, but they were still very pretty.

"Try these," she smiled, holding them out to Jeanne.

The girl looked incredulous. "For me?" she whispered, her dirty little hand coming out.

The shoes fitted her well enough, and if they pinched here and there, she hardly noticed, her face shining with pride and delight as she tottered about in them.

Anna gave her some of the other clothes, too. She was much plumper than Maria, but she could let out the seams of the gowns. The girl went humming away, her arms full, to stow them safely in the dirty attic she shared with the other maids.

Anna called up the senior of the maids and gave her the rest of the things to share between her companions, warning her not to let them interfere with Jeanne. "I owed her a service," she said, in explanation of her interest in the girl. She knew what jealousies bred among the servants and wished to spare Jeanne these if she could.

Over the next few weeks she saw a great deal of Yves. He was their most frequent visitor, always bringing her little gifts of wine, new books or flowers. She played to him, in the salon, while he leaned over the piano dreamily, his face softened into tender lines.

She was totally at ease with him. Once Yves asked if she had seen her assailant again, and she retailed the incident when she had seen Charles Baccoult outside the house, and his odd disappearance.

"Perhaps Maria's great beauty silenced his anger," said Yves, wryly.

Anna shook her head eagerly. "Oh, no, I am sure he was not a man to be influenced by that!"

Yves glanced at her, one brow lifting. She blushed, realizing how she must have sounded to him.

"What are you making today?" he asked, changing the subject, with a glance at the embroidery on her lap.

She spread it out. "A cushion cover." He touched it with one finger, admiring the design of squirrels, acorns and oak leaves. She was making a set of them for the chairs—illustrating the seasons of the year.

"Busy little creature," he teased, with a warm glance. "You are like a squirrel yourself." He touched her long chestnut hair. "Even to your bushy tail!"

Anna blushed and nervously pulled at the green silk. After a pause, his large, capable hand covered hers, and she looked up, eyes enormous.

"Anna," he said slowly, "I have received a summons home to Dijon. I must go. And it will be a long time before I return to Paris."

"Oh, what a pity!" She responded with warm disappointment, never thinking what impression she conveyed. "I shall miss you!"

The gray eyes were attentive. "Shall you, Anna?"

Her eyes were held by his, slightly puzzled by his deep tone, but smiling. "Of course I shall—we are friends, are we not?"

"Friends?" He smiled crookedly. "I want rather more than that of you, Anna. Will you marry me?"

She stared at him, eyes widening. "Yves!"

"I do not dress it up, Anna, in pretty words. My profession has taught me to despise them. Honestly and with deep feeling, I ask you to be my wife. I love you. I thought you must know."

"No, I . . . oh!" Her disjointed words brought a faint smile from him, but the gray eyes were alert to every change in her mobile face.

"I realize," he said, "that there are many obstacles. Our different nationalities, our different ages . . ."

"Oh, no," she said quickly, sensing that he was sensitive on this matter. "The difference in our ages does not weigh with me."

He flushed, looking relieved. "All the same, Anna, I am twice your age. It must be a barrier."

"Twice? What nonsense," she said lightly. "You hardly look more than thirty!"

"I am thirty-seven," he said abruptly.

She smiled at him. "You wear your years so lightly, Yves. One would never suspect. If I loved you, I should not care what age you were."

He drew back. "Ah! If you loved me?"

She stood up, letting her embroidery fall to the floor. He watched her tall, graceful figure as she walked around the room.

"I am very fond of you. You know that. You have always been so kind to me, your friendship has come to mean so much . . ." She twisted her hands helplessly, staring at the floor. "I am sorry, really sorry, but I cannot love you, Yves. My feelings are so different! Warm, sisterly . . ."

He broke into quick speech, very flushed. "I suspected, of course, that you did not feel as I do. Your manner, your reactions, were not those of love. But I hoped that . . ." he began to stammer, running his words together incoherently, "taking into account your situation . . . your lack of dowry . . . the home I could provide . . . every comfort and tenderness . . ."

"Oh, Yves, you are such a dear, kind man," she said unhappily. "How I wish I could. But . . ."

With a deep sigh, he shrugged. "I see. Hush, not a word more. We will forget the whole subject. I came, you know, prepared for a refusal. I must go. If you are ever near Dijon, call upon me, Anna . . ."

He took her hand, kissed it with a passion that surprised and shook her, then with a choked sound hurried from the room.

In the succeeding days she felt an emptiness. Yves had become her closest friend during their brief acquaintance, and she wished fervently that for him that closeness had not become love, since it had meant the end of all possible friendship.

How had she been so blind? She saw now various little hints which she had ignored or misunderstood. Looks, phrases, gestures, now revealing his growing feelings, but at the time not understood.

She, who had always known at once when a man fell in love with Maria, had entirely misread the signs when she, herself, was the object.

Anna was surprised to find herself missing Maria, too. They had been thrown together, for lack of other friends, and she had not realized in how many ways her waking hours depended upon Maria for amusement or employment.

She was a quiet, solitary girl, fond of reading, drawing, sewing, music: all quiet tasks. She looked to Maria for the diversity her own nature did not offer. Maria, always busy, talking, growing cross, flirting, needing flattery or sympathy, arousing reproof or regret, or wholehearted admiration for her beauty.

Anna realized that life had lost its savor. She had never been dull with Maria on hand to stir her into laughter or irritation.

Her uncle was busy, winding up his business contacts in France. The hours hung heavily for Anna. She turned more and more to Jeanne for company.

Mère Conjou permitted Jeanne to attend Anna as a personal maid, and the girl learned quickly how to perform the various duties Anna set her. Cheerful, eager, willing, she was grateful for the chance to acquire all the necessary skills for her projected future with her brother.

Anna was concerned when Jeanne came to her one morning, with red eyes, to say that her brother had sent for her. He was very ill. Anna comforted her, promised comforts for Jacques and filled the girl's skimpy purse with coins.

Jeanne did not return that night, nor the next day. Mère Conjou sent a letter, by hand, demanding that Jeanne come back or at least give some reason for her absence. There was no reply.

At Anna's suggestion, the scullion lad from the kitchen was sent to inquire at the wine shop. He returned with the news that the shop was shuttered, and he had had no reply to his knocking. The neighbors knew nothing, either.

"She's run off," grunted Mère Conjou, spitting on the floor. "Lazy little slut! These country girls are all the same. Come to Paris with one idea in their head. A fine gentleman tips his hat, and away they go! I dare say she sleeps between silk sheets tonight. Long may it last! A few months, and she'll be on the same old slide as the rest! Pretty face spoiled. Health gone. Hah! They make me sick! I warned her! She can't say I didn't!"

Anna could not believe it. The child had been too innocent. What fine gentleman would pursue those rosy cheeks, that cheerful, healthy child-like face?

And if one had, she was convinced, Jeanne's reaction would have been to run in horror back to the safety of the servants' attic.

But as the days passed, and no word came, she grew more and more concerned.

At last, she made up her mind to visit the shop herself, and see what she could find out.

She wore her oldest, most shabby cloak, with a large, all-concealing hood, and made her way across Paris on the rumbling wagon which served the poor. Seated on rough wooden benches they jolted along, in a spitting rain. Anna was glad of the excuse to keep her face hidden beneath a hood.

When at last she found the narrow, dirty little street which Jeanne had described, the shop was shuttered and desolate. The stale odor of cheap wine hung about it still.

Anna knocked loudly on the door, nervously glancing behind her for fear of attracting attention. The other houses seemed to watch her, breathing a menacing rush of foul air, their roofs crumbling, their doors sagging.

The door opened. A small, hunched woman peered closely at her before allowing her to enter, and at once putting up thick wooden bars across the door without a word.

"What do you want, *citoyenne?*" she growled.

"I wish to see Jeanne," said Anna, keeping her hood about her.

"Jeanne?" The woman wiped her hands slowly on her shabby gown. "Upstairs. She has a fever. She caught it from her brother."

Jeanne's silence was now explained. But why had she not sent word to the house? "Is she very ill?" Anna asked the old woman, who shrugged with wry indifference.

"Who knows? She has no money for doctors. I have my own living to earn. I cannot afford to nurse her and catch her fever. She caught it herself from nursing her brother."

"You mean they are both ill up there?" Anna was horrified at the other woman's flat dismissal of the two human beings who shared the same roof.

"He's dead," the old woman said casually. "She spent her last sou on his burial." Her wrinkled face twitched. "More fool her! I warned her. Who'll pay for your coffin, I asked. She looked ill from the second day she was here—he died that morning. She was white, shivering. I put it down to shock, but next day she was worse."

Anna winced, thinking of the girl's rosy, child's face. Pity stabbed like a knife. "And you have left her up there alone ever since?" she demanded, her voice sharp with reproof.

The woman looked offended. "I rent a room here —that doesn't make me her keeper."

"If you had sent word to us we would have done something," Anna said angrily.

"Oh, all very fine, but it was none of my business. It doesn't pay to be a good Samaritan these days. We've learnt to look the other way when there's trouble." She pointed up the stairs. "She's in the first room on the landing." And the old woman silently disappeared down the passage.

Anna stood, staring up the narrow flight of stairs. It was more like a ladder, in fact, with planks of wood nailed to a thin handrail against the wall.

She slowly made her way up the stairs to the wooden landing. Two doors opened from it. She took the first, pushing open the door after knocking.

A musty scent arose, partly stale air, partly wood rot. A tumbled bed took up most of the bare chamber. Jeanne lay on it, her body tossed down as though someone had dropped her there.

Her thick fair curls were matted and uncombed. Her cotton nightgown stained and crumpled. Her once rosy face the color of the dust which lay over the room.

In the pale light filtering down through the grimy small window, Anna saw that the girl's eyes were open, staring up at the cobwebbed rafters.

Death once seen is never forgotten. Anna walked to the bed, her eyes pricking with tears, and touched Jeanne's cheek with the back of her hand. It was icy cold.

She closed her eyes, a sob forcing its way up her chest, then forced herself to begin the tasks which must be done on these occasions.

When she was ready to leave, the chamber lay in neat order. The bed had been made. Jeanne lay with her arms crossed on her breast, her hair combed, her face clean. Anna draped the cleanest sheet over her and stood back, trembling, a cold perspiration breaking out on her spine.

At least no stranger should see the girl as she had seen her. In death one should have dignity.

When she went downstairs, the old woman hobbled out of her den. Anna coldly informed her of Jeanne's death, and the old woman crossed herself. Anna gave her some money, asking her to make arrangements for Jeanne's burial, and promising to send someone to make sure everything was properly arranged.

She would also have to write to Jeanne's family, she thought, sadly, and let them know that they had lost both children at once. She went quickly out of the house, eager to shake off the misery which pervaded it and breathe clean air once more.

She walked quickly, hardly noticing where she was going, her thoughts preoccupied with images of death. How brief a taste of joy the girl had been granted. Such a short life! She remembered Jeanne talking about her pet goose, Chou-Chou, whom she had had to leave behind. She had wept over the bird so short a time ago, and now had died with no one to weep for her.

In a secure corner Jeanne had carefully placed the red shoes which Anna had given her, so that from her sickbed she could admire them. Tawdry, shabby, gaudy objects, they seemed now a symbol of the waste of life. They were all that remained of Jeanne in Paris. Before she had finished tidying the room, Anna had gently slid them on to the girl's cold feet.

She suddenly came back to her surroundings with a start as she turned a corner and found herself unable to go further. A large crowd blocked the end of the street. They were crowding around a bakery, shouting and waving their fists. She heard a confused babble, out of which the one word Bread soared frequently.

A stone smashed into the bolted door. She heard the sound of wood splintering. One ragged, wild-eyed man threw himself at the door, thumping on it, shouting. Behind him swirled the others, faces contorted.

Anna drew back in dismay, pulling her hood forward to cover her face. She hastily looked behind her, but her way back was already blocked by the running of others from the houses around.

Whatever had caused the incident, the grapevine had already spread word of it. It took very little to spark a riot in the slums of Paris.

The long, winding street was filled with sweating bodies. Above them the gabled roofs rose to the blue sky. The sun hung there, like a bronze coin. The rain which had come earlier in the day had damped down the pavements and washed away some of the sewage from the gutters, but the heat pouring up from the crowd filled the air with thick odors.

"Bread! Give us bread!" The voices chanted furiously.

She saw a woman with a thin, ragged child in her arms, blue lips drawn back in hunger and despair, her starving eyes fixed on the bakery as though upon heaven.

A brawny, muscled fellow in torn shirt and breeches bellowed from the front of the crowd. "We know you have food in there, Basin! Must we starve while you stuff your belly?"

Anna had never known what it was to feel panic mounting in a tidal wave. She shrank back and back, trembling in every limb. She wanted to run, but there was nowhere to run to, and her legs had turned to water.

She found herself backing against the walls of the house behind her. Like a rat in a trap, she looked everywhere for a means of escape, her ears and eyes battered into confusion.

A door creaked open suddenly. A hand grabbed at her cloak and pulled her inside. She stumbled over the threshold, shaking violently.

The change from fear to relief was too much for her to be able to do more than whisper, "Thank you . . . oh, thank you . . ." again and again.

She leaned against the passage wall, recovering herself, her skin ice-cold with fear. Gradually she became aware of what was around her. She was in a dark and narrow passage. The light was too dim for her to see or be seen with any clarity, but she guessed from his height that her rescuer was a man.

His patience while she returned to normal argued some degree of kindness, so she felt no fear of him. He took firm hold of her wrist, his fingers cool and gentle, and led her along a passage into a small room, where an old woman sat beside a low fire watching a steaming pot.

Anna halted in the doorway, looking across the room, and the old woman gave her a toothless grin.

The red glow of the fire sufficiently illuminated the room for her to be able to see her rescuer. She looked at him now, with grateful curiosity, only to sway on her feet, her heart thudding in renewed panic, as she recognized him.

Seeing that she was on the point of fainting, he exclaimed, and pushed back her hood, beginning to undo the laces of her cloak, only to halt in his turn, his face darkening, as he recognized her.

"You!"

The harsh, bitter voice was like an echo from a nightmare. She leaned away from him, staring with the fixity of a cornered animal.

Her rescuer was Charles Baccoult.

Four

He made no move to touch her. After a long moment, while she shrank away in passive terror, he made a grimace of self-derision.

"Oh, do not gape at me with that white face! I do not intend to harm you, girl!"

She still waited, tense, her eyes fixed on his face. It seemed she was out of the frying pan into the fire. Recalling his violence when they first met she could not relax.

He turned away, his lip twisting in that now familiar fashion, and spoke in rapid French to the old woman by the fire, who cackled and replied with a mumble.

Anna's brain seemed to have slowed. Or else they spoke some patois of the streets. For she understood nothing of what passed between them. But the quick glance of the old woman at her was full of sly amusement, and she suspected a joke at her expense. In some odd way this eased her fear.

Charles Baccoult had pulled out a roughly hewn stool from beneath the table against the wall. Dusting it with his own kerchief, he gestured to her to seat herself.

She hesitated, looking uneasily at the door.

"Oh," he shrugged, baring his teeth, "leave by all means, if you wish. I am not going to stop you. But it will be some time before those men out there have finished their business, and what you would see would not be pretty. Pierre Basin has never been popular with the local people. He was too fat and too well fed. Now he is detested. And men with empty bellies take cruel revenge."

She shuddered and without a word sank down on to the stool. The old woman took down a wooden bowl from the shelf above the fire and filled it with a steaming liquid. She blew on it vigorously and offered it to Anna with a grin.

Anna forced a nervous smile and accepted it. She looked at the contents with secret distaste. She was far from hungry. The shocks she had suffered had taken away her appetite, but even had she been starving, she doubted if she would have been able to force herself to eat the mess she saw in the bowl.

An oily liquid, thickened with root vegetables crudely diced, in which floated scraps of yellow meat fat and strips of cabbage, it gave off a strong odor.

Charles Baccoult, watching her, leaned over and hissed, "Eat, *citoyenne!* She offers you her hospitality!"

With a trembling hand she lifted the bowl and sipped. The soup was boiling hot and scalded her tongue. It was not, however, she found to her surprise, inedible. She sipped again, more slowly, and felt her stomach relax as the warmth of the soup reached it.

The little room was like a cavern, dark and shadowy; the old woman, seated over her fire, was a witch, stirring her cauldron, her wrinkled features illumined by the red glare from the flames.

There was a nightmare quality about the situation. She wondered if she would wake up and find herself at home in her bed. Even now, as her fear subsided, her lids were drooping, her body growing heavy, she was yawning.

Exhausted by the events she had just suffered, she was growing unbearably sleepy with the effect of the heat and the darkness.

She finished the soup and whispered, *"Merci, cito-yenne!"* Her voice trembled and she bit her lip.

The crumpled old features stretched in a toothless smile which, she suddenly realized, was meant to be kind. "Good, eh? Good soup?"

"Very good," Anna whispered, aware in every nerve of Charles Baccoult's dark gaze on her face.

He took the bowl from her and replaced it, unwashed, on the shelf. Anna sat, her hands in her lap, wondering how much longer she would have to wait here.

The room was very still. The old woman's head drooped forward on to her chest; she began to snore, mouth open, the wispy hairs on her upper lip blowing in and out with the whistling of her breath. The ash drifted down from the fire over her sabots.

Charles Baccoult moved his stool nearer, looking at Anna out of sardonic black eyes.

"Now, *citoyenne,* how do you come to be in the Faubourg Saint-Antoine, so far from your own fashionable quarter?"

"I was visiting a sick servant," she said nervously.

"You were doing what?" The sheer disbelief in his voice made her flush.

"My maid was sick. I visited her at her home in this quarter." The reality of Jeanne's death rushed over her again and she felt cold and sick. "She was dead when I got there!" she said miserably.

"And so you hurried away before you became infected yourself?" he sneered.

She was barely conscious of him, remembering Jeanne's dusty white face, the disorder and staleness of the room.

"I laid her out and left money for the funeral," she said on a quavering sigh.

He leaned forward, eyes narrowed. "You would not know how to begin," he retorted, eyes contemptuous.

"I saw it done when my grandmother died," she said, and her mind flashed back to the quiet upper room of her old home. There had been rain on the windows, the soft gentle sound of English summer rain soaking into the earth. A fire had burned in the hearth all night, but it had been allowed to sink by then, and she had watched it sifting through the grate, gray specks of ash floating on to the floorboards. They had forgotten her presence, busy around the bed, their women's voices hushed, and she had watched them in the calm, bewildered despair of childhood.

She knew now why the dusty look of Jeanne's face had so deeply disturbed her, bringing up old memories long buried.

He was still staring at her, but the hostility had faded, giving way to a puzzled curiosity.

She started, becoming aware of him again. "I never forgot," she said huskily, glancing down at her hands.

"One doesn't," he agreed softly.

There was another silence. She could feel his eyes on her, and wondered what he was thinking.

"Louis has left Paris, *citoyenne*," he suddenly said, in a harsh voice.

She did not hear the deliberate whipping-up of his anger, only that now-familiar thread of violence. "Where has he gone?" she stammered.

"He has joined the army. Thrown up his career—it is another form of suicide, of course."

"I am sorry," she said lamely, not knowing how to answer the accusation in his voice. He must hate all the members of her family, she knew. There was nothing to be said in the face of the wrong Maria had done his brother.

"Sorry?" His tone rose angrily. "No wonder they say the English are a nation of hypocrites! Your cousin ruins the boy for a selfish whim, and you say you are sorry?"

"What else can I say?" she asked in desperation. "I am not responsible for my cousin. I am sorry this has happened, but there was never anything I could do to stop it."

"Women are happiest when they give pain," he said, ignoring her. "They love to humble those who love them. Give a man a whip and only the cruel ones will use it. But give a woman beauty, and she will use it as a weapon every time."

"You are unfair to my sex," she protested, with burning cheeks. "You cannot generalize from one woman to all women."

"I have not done so," he said coldly. "I speak from experience of more than one cold and beautiful woman. I did not need to speak to your cousin to understand her—one glance sufficed. I am not a callow boy to be blinded and misled by golden curls. I saw beneath the pretty shell to the emptiness within, *citoyenne*."

She looked at him sideways. "Why did you go away without coming to the house?" she dared ask.

His black eyes flashed with sardonic amusement. "Did you wait in terror for my knock on the door?"

he asked mockingly. "I pictured the two of you trembling like rabbits at the approach of the fox."

Anna gave him an indignant look. "We were meant to feel like that, were we?"

He shrugged. "I intended to beard your cousin and have it out with her, but at the last moment I lost my zeal. Your look of horror as you caught sight of me took away my appetite for revenge. I have always thought it a petty motive, in any case. So I just walked away. I imagined you would have put the fear of God into your cousin, anyway—so my visit was hardly needed any longer."

She looked at him critically. His face in the red glow of the fire was all dark hollows and stark angles. The arrogant long nose, strong jaw and high, fleshless cheekbones magnetized the eye. He was a man to arouse curiosity. Such violence combined with such gentleness was rare.

"Would you kill yourself for the sake of a woman?" she asked.

"No," he snapped, "but I might kill her!"

Yes, she thought, she could believe that. Aloud she said, "Maria is not entirely to blame, you know. Few men commit suicide for love. Maria was wrong to encourage him, of course, but she could not have known he would go to pieces. Louis was too vulnerable."

He laughed curtly. "I see it is now to be Louis's fault! How like a woman to find another scapegoat."

"I was not looking for a scapegoat. I was trying to be just."

"Women do not recognize justice when they see it," he said. "They always blame someone else. They cannot accept responsibility." He stood up. "We can leave now, I think. They will have done their worst and slunk back to their rat-holes, poor creatures, to gnaw on wood instead of the bread they need." He threw a coin on the table. *"Mère* Gagneau will find it when she wakes. Come!"

Baffled, she looked from him to the old woman. "This is not your home, then?"

His lean face tightened. "No," he said derisively, "I am poor by your standards, *citoyenne,* but I live better than this. I am a doctor, as I think I told you, and some of my patients live in these slums. *Mère* Gagneau is one. This damp hovel has given her swollen joints and the English chest complaint. She wheezes like a pair of rusty bellows in winter."

She followed him down the passage. He motioned her to wait while he looked outside to make sure the road was clear.

He turned and gestured that it was safe. "I will escort you home," he told her brusquely, "and you should not come into this district again alone."

"I must see that Jeanne is decently buried," she protested. "She has no relatives in Paris. She cannot be interred without a single mourner."

He looked at her, frowning. "What a baffling mixture you are! Send a servant—I expect you have several who would be glad of a few hours off. Next time you might not be so lucky. Had I seen your face before I dragged you into *Mère* Gagneau's hovel, I might have left you to suffer the consequences of your folly."

She was beginning to know him, and this statement did not alarm her.

She shuddered as they passed the bakery. The place had been smashed open. The door hung, broken, from the hinge. The street was full of splintered wood. A woman with bruised face and torn clothing wept, lying against a wall, a whining child plucking at her arm.

Charles muttered a string of curses, his dark face

violent. She could feel the rage in him. "That might have happened to you," he told her. He shot her a savage glance. "Perhaps you think that women will not feel the degradation of being violated by brutal men. You gently bred females are so much more sensitive than your low-class sisters!"

She was hurt by that remark. "If you are so moved," she said fiercely, "why didn't you stop them? You knew what was going on!"

She was sorry immediately, seeing his face go white. "Because," he said starkly, "I am a coward. I knew the odds. One man against a hundred. What do you think would have been the result?"

"I'm sorry," she whispered.

His look lashed her. "You make a habit of it," he said.

At the end of the road a figure lay sprawled, a rope around its neck, face down in the mud. Anna swayed, sickness boiling inside her.

Charles slid an arm around her and made her walk on. "He's dead," he said tautly, "but the men who killed him are still starving. They will take longer to die, and it will be far more painful."

Below the anger which ravaged his face there burned a pity which was like rage in its despair of finding release, a pity directed both at the baker and his family, and the men who in their own despair had done these terrible things.

She had seen this emotion in so many others. In the cadaverous features of René Lagrett, with his manic bursts of laughter and his wild grief, who contorted himself with the sheer frustration of finding any escape from the human situation of his fellow-low Parisians.

Outside her lodgings they parted. She tentatively held out her hand, her eyes grave.

He looked down at it as though it were some strange, alien object.

"We are not polite acquaintances, *citoyenne*. We are enemies. Your family have done mine a great wrong." He shrugged. "I am not a Christian. I do not hate on principle. I am an honest atheist. I know better than to blame the snake for its bite, or the cat for its claws. But I avoid them when I can, so I will not take your hand, *citoyenne*. Today I saved your life—let that wash out my violence towards you at our first meeting. We will part on equal terms. But enemies." He touched his hat, bowed, and vanished down the street.

She watched him with straining eyes until he had passed from sight.

She had never known a man like him. So wild, so violent, so oddly kind. Like all quiet people she was drawn to natures opposite to her own. Running like a gentle stream through dark valleys, she was drawn to his passion, like a moth to a flame, eyes dazzled, heart hungry. As a slow river rushes to the sea, she felt impelled to think of him, as the days passed, with curiosity and intense interest.

She watched with dismay, that week, the sadness and heaviness of her uncle's step as he came into the salon each evening. Many of his friends were vanishing: some into prison, some dying on the guillotine, some conscripted and others, no doubt, afraid to be seen in the company of foreigners who were under such a black cloud at the moment.

Maria wrote to them from Geneva, brief, gay letters describing her social life, and these were all that Sir Henry lived for now. He was hurrying to finish winding up his affairs, but found that many trusted friends proved difficult now that he was trying to withdraw his funds instead of investing them.

It became clear that he would lose a great deal by leaving France.

All over France the voices of moderation were falling silent. The Girondins were finished. The more powerful voices of fanaticism triumphed. The radiance which had seemed to surround the city when they first arrived had vanished. Rumor, suspicion and fear had clouded the bright dawn of liberty. Midnight arrests grew more common. The prisons overflowed. Massacre, murder, brutality were daily events.

Autumn was upon them, a long, slow golden autumn. The Seine ran like a river of shining metal beneath the trees. Anna dreamt of England's misty autumn mornings, longing to wake and find herself there, under the burnished elms, where mushrooms sprouted in damp grass, and the spiders spun dewy webs from bush to bush.

It was agony now to awake, and hear the slow rumble of carts, the rattle of French voices, like musket fire in her ears. She would never grow used to the rapidity with which French people spoke. The slow Kent drawl sounded, by comparison, like the mumbling of a sleepwalker.

One evening, in early October, Sir Henry announced that his business was finished, and they could go home at once. They were to travel to Switzerland for Maria first.

"Oh, how glad I am," said Anna joyfully.

He smiled, wiping his forehead. "Aye, so am I, m'dear. But gracious heavens, I am hot! I have been everywhere in such a great hurry that I have fair worn myself out. I have the headache, too, but what can I expect, overworking like this?"

She looked anxiously at him. "You do not look well. I hope you have not taken some disease. Perhaps you should stay in bed tomorrow."

"I cannot take to my bed now, Anna. We must leave at dawn. The rumors are growing. I dare delay no longer. As it is, I shall lose considerably by leaving. A large amount is still outstanding, but I fear if I wait I shall lose everything!"

"You will be sad to leave France, Uncle," she said gently.

He sighed. "Aye, I shall. But better to leave it with my head still on my shoulders, eh?"

As Anna lay in bed she wondered what memories of France she would carry with her. It was sad to end their life here in this fashion. They had been so happy here once.

Try as she might, one face dominated her sleepy mind. Charles Baccoult's wild countenance would haunt her for a long time, she suspected.

She dreamt of Charles Baccoult. They sat together in that firelit cavern of a room, his face close to hers, and she vainly tried to make him listen as she explained how sorry she was for what had happened to Louis.

He lifted his hand and thumped it down upon the table, shouting to drown her words.

The thuds grew louder, the shouts more fierce. Suddenly she was wide awake, and knew it was no dream.

The sounds she had woven into her dream were real. Someone was demanding entrance to the house, pounding on the door with muskets.

She knew at once what it meant. Sir Henry had left their escape too late. They were to be arrested.

She hurriedly dressed, her fingers fumbling in the darkness. She dared not pause to light a candle.

She finished just as the door was flung open. A squat, ragged soldier marched in, barking aggressively.

She understood him, although her brain was cloudy with sleep, and moved towards the door.

He gripped her arm, twisting it behind her back, so that she cried out in pain, and pushed her down towards the salon.

Stumbling into the middle of the candle-lit room, with her chestnut hair tumbling down over her shoulders, eyes blinking in the sudden light, she looked anxiously for her uncle.

He hurried to her, his face drawn. "My poor child, they have not harmed you?"

"No, no," she reassured. Indeed, she was more concerned for him than for herself.

His shirt was unbuttoned, his jacket flung hastily around him. He wore no cravat. His hair stood on end, like the quills of a porcupine, giving him a cross, untidy appearance, which would in other circumstances have made her smile. He was very flushed, but whether from sleep, or temper, she could not tell.

"No talking, except to me!" barked a small gentleman in a dark jacket across whose breast was draped the tricolor sash of the republic.

"Jack in office," muttered Sir Henry in English, grinding his teeth smoothly.

Anna smiled.

The little man glared at them both. "I am a commissary of the revolutionary committee of this section," he stated in a harsh voice. Anna looked at him closely, and decided that he was forcing himself to be unpleasant. It was not in his nature. The strained look around his pale eyes betrayed him.

He held up a large parchment. "I have here the decree of the Convention, ordering the arrest of all British citizens." He coughed. "Do you wish me to read it to you?"

Sir Henry eyed the seals on the parchment. "No,"

he retorted with icy dignity. "We are prepared to obey the law."

The three soldiers withdrew to the passage, where the servants were gathered. The commissary nodded approvingly, his manner relaxing now that the soldiers had gone. "You are very wise," he told Sir Henry. "I beg you will compose yourselves. If you are innocent of any political crimes against the republic you have nothing to fear."

How could he lie so glibly, Anna thought sadly? She watched the perspiration on his brow, his nervous mannerisms. Poor little man, he is more terrified than we are!

"I will now take a procés-verbal," he said with relief, sliding into the routine processes of the law. "Do not be alarmed, *citoyenne*," he told Anna. "This is merely a verbal statement for our files. We want to know how long you have been in Paris, how old you are . . . you understand?"

She whispered that she did, and the questions began. They were all innocuous, except one which demanded to know the exact amount of personal property, including money.

"You may take with you as much clean linen as you can carry easily," he told them brusquely. "The rest of your property is seized by the nation." He looked quickly at Sir Henry. "That is why you were asked for a list of your possessions. Do you wish to see the relevant part of the decree? If you declare openly all you possess, you may get it back later." His tone sounded very doubtful, however, and he did not quite meet their eyes.

Sir Henry shrugged. "I understand." His voice was full of bitter contempt, and the commissary flushed.

"Come," he barked, once more the military bully. "We have no time to waste. Fetch what you need at once."

As they left the servants jeered and some citizens in the street spat at them. The commissary ordered the soldiers to clear a path without delay, and with rough indifference they used their muskets to knock the observers out of the way.

They were taken to a local committee room which was crowded with soldiers and commissaries. Every half hour a guard entered, conducting more English prisoners.

There were few women among them, since most of them had already left the country. They seemed very calm and composed: read newspapers or dozed quietly on their benches, with as little fuss as though they were waiting for a coach.

From time to time one of the soldiers burst into song, or shouted blasphemies, threatening the prisoners with the guillotine. Many of them appeared to be drunk.

Anna sat in silence. She was very much afraid. The roughness of the guards, the liberty allowed them by their officers, made her fear what was to follow. They were helpless, impotent.

Her uncle was flushed and restless, moving constantly, his eyes fever-bright. He is angry, she thought anxiously, and prayed he would not endanger his life by retorting the next time a soldier insulted them.

A commissary came to nail a document to the wall next to her, and she asked him how much longer they were to be held there.

Glancing round to make sure they were not observed, he whispered that they would wait until morning to be moved.

"And then?"

"Then?" He shrugged. "The Luxembourg, perhaps. Or the Madelonettes. If you are lucky it will be the Luxembourg. They have big, fine apartments there, with beds. The Madelonettes is already over-crowded. The prisoners sleep on their feet."

She shuddered. "Good God!"

He automatically lifted a hand to cross himself, then snatched it down, trembling. "Ah, little *cito-yenne*," he whispered, "God is sleeping."

"If we had only left Paris yesterday," she mourned.

He shook his head. "You would have been brought back. Do you know the penalty for harbor-ing *les Anglaises*? Ten years in prison! Someone would have caught you."

When he had gone, she closed her eyes. The hard wooden bench was uncomfortable, but the room was hot, and the smoking brazier filled the air with an acrid scent. She grew sleepy enough to forget her discomfort.

When she opened her eyes again it was cold, gray dawn. The scene had a new desolation. The soldiers moved them along roughly. *"À bas les Anglaises . . ."* they grunted, poking them with their muskets.

They were a rough, tattered collection, carrying outdated weapons and bearing themselves with swag-gering insolence. They were untrained, undisciplined and brutal. Compared to them, the commissary were a credit to the republic.

She looked round at her uncle, and her heart dropped like lead. He was weary-eyed, and drawn about the mouth. A fine dew of perspiration covered his temples.

But he smiled at her, and she was inexpressibly comforted by his silent affection.

They were pushed into a coach along with some other prisoners and two sullen guards, who watched them with hostility. Two other guards walked along-side the coach, which moved at a snail's pace.

The streets were already busy with people, who

either stared with dull indifference or raised fists and shouted.

She looked at her uncle with pity. It must be hard for him to bear all this. He had come to France with such idealism and hope, believing it to be the dawn of a new age for the world. How far those hopes had fallen in this last year!

She suddenly recognized the Rue d'Enfer, and guessed that they were being taken to the Luxembourg, once a famous royal palace, now used as a prison for the very people who had once been proud to be seen there.

Sir Henry was shivering violently. Anna leaned forward in distress, but the guard barked, "Stay where you are!"

She sank back, sighing.

The coach rumbled to a halt. They were pushed out and began to climb the steps of the Luxembourg. A waiting crowd seethed around them, threatening and insulting those nearest with a sort of ferocious gaiety. They were enjoying themselves. It had become the cheapest form of entertainment in Paris, the harassment of arriving prisoners, and was only second in popular acclaim to the spectacle of an execution.

One or two men squatted on the ground, devouring a sparse breakfast with the ravenous haste of dogs, in case someone tried to snatch their crust away. Through their threadbare clothes Anna could see the grime of unwashed skin. Their cheeks and lips were livid with cold.

The guards pushed their prisoners on at a fast pace, and soon they were climbing the broad stairs to the apartments set aside for them, above the former rooms of state.

It was strange to walk, bullied and driven like sheep, under walls still hung with the rich tapestries which had once pleased the eyes of the kings of France.

The keeper of the Luxembourg prison, Citizen Benoit, greeted them on the landing. A neat, mild man, he gave each little group of people a few quiet words, his voice gentle, concerned.

He was known for the humanity of his regime at the Luxembourg. Vainly he had struggled to maintain decent standards of treatment in the prison, doing what little he could in the face of vicious brutality from the military.

When he came to Anna, supporting Sir Henry on her arm, he looked at her with distress.

"Ah, *citoyenne,* it is sad to see the young imprisoned. A prison is no place for nicely bred young girls. But I will find you the best apartment I can!" His smile was gently wry. "Yes, princes of the blood royal were proud to sleep in the rooms I offer you. Some of them have slept here less happily, I fear."

As they followed him down a dark, narrow passage, Sir Henry stumbled, and Benoit gave him a pitying glance, and murmured, "Bear up, *mon ami!*"

The apartment into which they were shown was empty. The windows had been blocked up to the upper panes, which were barred, and the light was dim, but there was a table, two folding stools and a rather dirty old mattress on which were folded two blankets.

Benoit waved his hand around with pride. "Had you gone to the Madelonettes, *citoyenne,* you would not have found such luxury. For the moment you will have this apartment to yourself, but I may have to place others with you later today. You must have influential friends. Only prisoners of importance are put into my care, and I do what I can for them, within the limits of my duty to the state."

Anna thanked him, guiding her uncle to one of

the stools. He sank down without demur, dropping his head in his hand. Benoit looked anxiously at him.

"He is worn out, and no wonder! And you need rest, too, *citoyenne!* Do not fear disturbance. You will not be harmed here."

She thanked him with tears in her eyes. Now that they had escaped from the soldiers, she felt her courage leaving her, and longed for sleep.

Benoit hurried out, leaving the door unlocked. Anna helped her uncle to the mattress, covered him with the blankets and watched him for a few moments after he had fallen deeply asleep.

A tap on the door made her jump. She turned. A pale, smiling face was peering round the door.

"Good evening, Socrates!"

She blinked, wondering if this was some madman who had escaped from his cell.

Seeing her bewilderment, he bowed with all the exaggerated courtesy of the old regime.

"All the apartments have been bestowed with the names of great heroes," he explained, coming into the room. "Your chamber is named Socrates. If you look, you will see it inscribed upon the door." He gave her an ironic glance. "We live in a heroic society, you see, my dear Mademoiselle."

The title made her start. It was so long since she had heard it. Again the newcomer read her mind. He intoned, with magnificent dignity, "I reject the title of citizen, Mademoiselle. I am the Vicomte de Panerllon. My ancestors fought for France for six centuries. I need no rabble to confer upon me the name citizen!"

Anna was speechless. Such wild pride in this grim place was only to be marveled at. For far less had men gone to the guillotine.

Then he shrugged, deriding his own pride. "Well, I am now inhabiting the apartment Brutus—a fellow

I never admired. The betrayal of a friend should not be required by the state! But, however, I came to explain to you how our little society here works. Our apartments lead into this passage. During the evening our doors remain unlocked so that we may visit each other. We have formed a miniature republic of our own. Each helps the other. We have to send out for our food, since of course none is provided. Each has his task. One sweeps the floor, another lays the fire."

Anna listened, smiling. Then she wondered how they were to obtain food. All their money had been seized. How were they to live without money?

"The Vicomtesse has a broom, which one may borrow, and an English lady has a kettle which never grows cold. Tomorrow you shall have English tea for breakfast." His delicate, pale face broke into a charming smile.

She thanked him warmly, and after a few more words, he left her to find what rest she could upon a corner of the mattress, wrapped in her cloak.

When she woke the room was full of brilliant sunshine. Her uncle still slept, his face covered. She crept across the room silently and stood on the table to look out of the uncovered part of the window.

She found herself looking out upon the famous gardens of the Luxembourg, on which had once been lavished the attentions of an army of royal gardeners.

It was early October. The stately trees still retained their leaves, which shone in the morning like living gold, turning in a slight breeze to dance up on the air. It was a shock to move one's eyes and see the broad terraces patrolled by soldiers in the ragged garb of the republic.

The skyline was fretted with gilded spires, standing out like the spears of an advancing army against

the wooded royal parks, and dreaming in the distance
the hills of Meudon, blue and misty, like the backcloth in a theater.

She stood for a while, gazing out, sighing, wondering if she would ever leave the confines of the
Luxembourg again.

Her uncle moved restlessly. She turned and glanced
at him, and something in his attitude disturbed her.
She hurried to him, bending to touch his forehead.

It was as dry and hot as desert sand. She knelt
and looked at him anxiously. His eyelids were puffy
and discolored, his lips parched and flaking. He
breathed heavily.

"Oh, no!" She wrung her hands, sobbing. "No,
you cannot be ill now, Uncle! You cannot be ill
now . . ."

Five

She ran to the door of the apartment. It was now locked, she found. She banged frantically on it, shouting for help, and after some time a guard opened the door and scowled at her.

"My uncle is ill!" she babbled in English. "Oh, help him. He is very ill . . ."

He stared at her uncomprehendingly.

She realized her error, and repeated herself, in French, her voice trembling. He stalked over to Sir Henry and looked at him. Then he left the room without a word, locking the door behind him.

Anna soaked her kerchief in some water from the jug provided on the table, and gently wiped her uncle's parched lips and temples.

A few moments later Benoit hurried in and inspected her uncle in his turn, his mild face anxious.

"I hope it is nothing infectious," he said nervously. "Contagion spreads in prison like fire . . ."

"A doctor," Anna begged. "Please, fetch a doctor to him . . ."

He hesitated. "Do you have a doctor of your own? Our prison doctor is not the most . . ." he glanced behind him and lowered his voice, "not the most amiable of men."

She bit her lip. Then, huskily, she said, "Dr. Charles Baccoult? Do you know of him?"

Benoit's face brightened. "But, of course! An excellent suggestion." He looked at her curiously. "He will come? He knows you?"

Firmly, to still her own uncertainty, Anna said, "He will come!" And crossed her fingers behind her back.

He had said, when they parted, that they were enemies. Yet he had been so oddly gentle, and his warmth towards the old hag by the fire had been enlightening. Anna believed he would come when he knew how serious their situation was here. She trusted in his heart.

Benoit had left the apartment door open. At a movement Anna turned eagerly, but it was the Vicomte once more.

He bowed ceremoniously. "I am very sorry to hear of your father's illness, Mademoiselle! I have brought you some tea. Are you hungry?"

She lifted her drooping head in eagerness. Tea! The very word made her heart lift. She took the delicate, hand-painted cup, breathing in the delicious fragrance with delight.

"Ah," sighed the Vicomte. *"Les Anglaises!* The mention of tea never fails to make them smile."

She thanked him warmly and he smiled. "Eat some bread, too, Mademoiselle. Madame la Vicomtesse begs you will do her the honor."

She looked incredulously at the dainty slice of bread. "She is too kind," she stammered.

Bowing, he withdrew. Anna broke the bread into quarters and ate one very slowly, hiding the other three in case her uncle should feel hungry later. Slowly she sipped the tea, making it last as long as possible. It seemed as though an eternity had passed since she last had a meal.

A bubble of hysterical laughter formed in her throat as she looked round the room. Here she sat, sipping tea from an exquisite piece of china, in this grim place! It seemed the height of lunacy.

Yet, somehow, the small kindness, the shred of normal life, made it possible for her to bear what was ahead. She could glimpse now the reason which made the Vicomte bravely maintain all his old habits of living in the face of the guillotine.

Her restless eye fell upon the tapestries which still covered the walls. Romantic landscapes: silver waterfalls, green hills and blue skies, gave the room a shabby beauty. When the wind blew they moved slightly, making the trees appear to wave, the birds seem to be spreading their wings. The fading colors only enhanced the illusion.

Suddenly Benoit entered, followed by Charles Baccoult. Anna felt her heart leap at the sight of his tall figure. She could not hide her look of joy and relief. He might call himself her enemy, but she trusted him more than any man she had ever met.

But he met her gaze coldly, giving no sign of recognition, and she felt as though he had slapped her face. At this moment, in her anxiety, to be so unkind! She had not expected it of him.

He went silently to Sir Henry and knelt down beside him. Anna and Benoit watched as he gently examined his patient, his long deft fingers probing and manipulating.

Anna's senses seemed doubly alive. She saw the tapestry glowing with color, saw the dust on the floor, the dancing golden motes which spread down the rays of the sun as they fell through the barred windows, saw the lines on Benoit's kindly, harassed face.

Charles straightened, frowning.

"Well, *citoyen docteur?*" Benoit asked nervously.

Before Charles could reply there was the sound of loud voices in the passage, the stamping of feet and the banging of muskets on doors.

Benoit was suddenly white. "Henriot!" He spoke the name with hoarse intensity.

Anna's heart sank. She had heard, as had all Paris, of Henriot, the notorious ex-valet who had become military commandant of the city. He was whispered to be half-mad, feared and hated even by those he served.

The apartment door was flung open, and in stalked a menacing figure, tricolor sash prominently displayed, brandishing a saber, his face contorted with drunken ferocity. A body of brutal, hard-faced soldiers followed him.

"*Mon général,*" said Benoit, hurrying to greet him, "how are you today?"

Henriot pushed him aside with grim, drunken contempt. He glared round the room. "And what have we here?" He advanced towards Anna, lip lifting in an interested sneer. "An English whore, is it? A pretty toy for Madame la Guillotine to play with!"

Anna, white to the lips, held herself still with difficulty, refusing to give way to fear, since this was plainly what would most delight this man.

He caught hold of her chin with one brutal hand, squeezing her bones until she felt they would crack. "Pretty!" he muttered. "Hey, Benoit, clear this room. I'll have private words with this whore of yours!"

His manic laughter was echoed, jackal-like, by his henchmen, who began to back out.

"Come closer," snarled Henriot, dragging her towards him, a hand on her waist.

"*Citoyen* Henriot," said a cold, authoritative voice from the other side of the room, "this Englishman has the smallpox."

Henriot spun on his heel, pushing Anna away. The marred lines of his stupid, cruel face tightened. "What's that? Oh, it is you, *citoyen docteur*. What did you say?"

"Smallpox," repeated Charles crisply. "The girl probably carries the contagion, too. They must be removed from this prison before it spreads."

Henriot swore viciously, stumbling towards the door, pushing Benoit out of his way. Benoit tremblingly followed him.

"Mon général," he pleaded, "what shall I do with them?"

Henriot turned on him a white, furious face. "Get them out of here! You heard the doctor. I want them out of here."

"But where shall I send them?" Benoit begged.

"To the devil," roared Henriot. "I'm off to have a bath in vinegar and herbs. If I am infected, I'll have your head, Benoit. You didn't tell me about the Englishman's illness. I'll have you for that!"

He stamped away after his terrified henchmen, his great rumbling voice coming back for a while; then silence succeeded.

Benoit looked at Charles, his hands spread in despair. "What am I to do, *citoyen docteur?*"

Charles picked up the delicate cup from which Anna had drunk her tea. With a casual gesture he smashed it to the floor. Benoit and Anna started and trembled.

"Everything they have used must be destroyed," he said, looking round the room.

"But what shall I do with them? Where can they go? Who will take them in?"

Charles rubbed his jaw. "I have an isolated house outside Paris," he said slowly. "I could take them— for a consideration."

Benoit's voice shook with eagerness. "I am sure

the Republic will be generous in its gratitude." He looked at Sir Henry. "Smallpox is . . ." he paused, as his voice shook, then went on, "It is a terrible disease." The skin around his eyes was livid. His lids blinked rapidly, his mouth twitched. He was obviously in extreme fear.

Charles took Benoit's arm and led him to the door. They talked in low voices for some time. Anna stared at the smashed pieces of the cup. Smallpox! She bit on her thumb, like a child, gasping back tears. If it did not kill, it left you horribly scarred. No wonder even Henriot had run from its presence as though from the guillotine.

She looked at her uncle's flushed face. He lay on his side, trembling violently, his arms and legs jerking convulsively.

Her own cheeks seemed wet and cool. She put up a wondering hand to touch them. Her fingers came away damp. She put one to her lips. Salt! Somewhere she could hear someone crying.

"Is it me who is crying?" she asked aloud.

"No, it is Madame la Vicomtesse," said Charles, at her elbow.

She looked up, startled. "Why?"

His hard mouth twisted derisively. He pointed to the broken cup. "She is mourning that! Benoit just told her it was broken. It was the last of a famous set made for her when she was married. Her last contact with the old life. Possessions assume a new importance in here—she weeps more than she did for her children. Then she could be brave, hoping to see them again. Now she knows her world has gone, and she clings to every slender thread that still binds her to her old life."

She shivered. "Poor woman." She felt very cold. "How happy this must make you," she observed to him conversationally. "Your revenge comes sooner than you expected. Smallpox! The worst disease for a woman! You must regret Maria's escape. That would have completed your pleasure."

"Get up and walk about," he said brusquely, gripping her elbow. "You will feel better for some exercise."

"My hands are so cold," she said childishly.

He took them without comment and rubbed them vigorously. She permitted him without movement, her face blank.

"I am taking you out tonight," he murmured. "You will be taken in a closed coach. If the people heard any rumors of an epidemic there would be more rioting!"

"What will happen to us?"

"Stop worrying," he ordered.

She began to laugh, hysterically. "We are given a death sentence and you tell me to stop worrying . . ."

He caught her by the shoulders, as he had before, but this time he shook her gently. "Stop that! You must remain calm!"

She bit her lip. "I . . . I am calm," she told him on a shaky breath.

He looked down at her oddly, still holding her, then pushed her away.

Her uncle muttered feverishly. "Maria, Maria!"

She ran to him, knelt down and caught his hand. His lids moved up. The whites of his eyes were bloodshot, the pupils contracted.

"My dearest child," he whispered.

Weeping, she lifted his hands and kissed them. The sunshine shimmered on her hair, turning the chestnut to gold. Sir Henry gave her a quavering smile.

"Maria, I thought you had gone away—you will not leave me, will you? Don't go away . . ."

"Never, never," she promised, realizing that in his

delirium he mistook her for her cousin. If it comforted and eased him she was happy.

Charles bent down and examined Sir Henry, frowning. She watched him, eyes anxious.

He straightened and pulled her to her feet. His black eyes probed hers. She wondered what he was thinking. His expression was enigmatic.

"Get some rest," was all he said, abruptly.

The day passed slowly. Once a charming French voice broke into an old folk song about a nightingale. Anna shivered. It was dream-like to sit here, in the darkening room, waiting. At the back of her mind loomed the menace of death, yet she found it hard to believe that she was soon to die. She felt too alive.

As soon as it was dark they were moved out, discreetly. Sir Henry was carried on a stretcher. Anna walked. Benoit saw them into a closed coach and murmured a regretful word or two before waving the driver on and slamming the door.

Two guards rode on the box to make sure they passed through each barrier without delay. At each checkpoint Anna heard them say, "Business of the state!" And then the coach rumbled on, through the sleeping streets of Paris. The vehicle was old and very slow. She jolted to and fro, head aching, listening to her uncle's heavy breathing, praying he would not die.

At dawn they were outside the city. Charles let down the leather window blind, and gray light filtered into the coach. Low clouds hung over the landscape. The birds were beginning to sing. Behind them the skies were already smoking with the glare from the city fires.

Paris was surrounded by small market gardens which supplied the needs of the city. In the misty light they could see rows of vegetables, fruit bushes, apple trees, some still heavy with unpicked fruit. Crows squawked and flapped among them, and a small ragged boy shouted and flung stones to drive them away, his bare feet sliding on the wet grass.

They were passing into deeper countryside, wooded and half empty. The coach ground to a halt before a tree-encircled house whose black beams proclaimed its age. A thin curl of blue smoke rose from the chimney. A cock crowed somewhere.

The guards carried Sir Henry into the house. Charles and Anna followed. The two men laid the stretcher in front of the house and without a word hurried back to the coach and drove off at once.

"They suspect something," said Charles sardonically. He called loudly, and the front door opened. A short, stocky man came out, in his shirt sleeves and breeches, a slice of dark bread in his hand.

He stared at Charles. "I thought I heard a coach! There you are, then, Charles!" His dark eyes moved to Anna, then to the stretcher. "What have we here?"

"Patients," Charles said laconically. "Give me a hand with this, will you, Jean-Claud?"

The other hurriedly swallowed the last of his bread. "Right," he grunted, bending.

Anna followed them into a dark, paneled hall, with a stone flagged floor and a great, open hearth. The air was redolent of something edible. She sniffed. It smelt like beef, she thought, but it could not be! Her stomach clenched convulsively with a dark hunger.

Charles and the other man carried her uncle up a winding wooden stair, very slowly. Anna made to follow them, but Charles nodded to her to wait.

"Gabrielle!" he called over his shoulder. "Attend to our guest!"

Anna's heart winced. She heard the clatter of sabots on the floor. A girl appeared at the end of a passage leading from the hall. She stared at Anna, eyes round.

She was a little shorter than Anna, shapely and sturdily built. Her coronet of thick, plaited hair was the color of ripe corn. Her eyes were a warm, melting brown. She wore the pale blue blouse and kilted apron of the peasant, her warm woolen hose just visible beneath the dark skirt.

"Did I hear Charles's voice?" she asked, in a slow country drawl. She looked Anna up and down, inspecting the shabby old cloak, the oddly elegant shoes which peeped from beneath her hem.

"Yes," Anna managed to say, her voice husky. Was this perhaps his wife? Or only his sister. She was shocked by the depths of her hope that it should be his sister.

The man called Jean-Claud came clumping down the stairs. He passed Anna without a word and vanished.

"You'd best come into the kitchen, then," Gabrielle said. Anna hung back. Was it wise to mix with other people, she wondered. Surely she would spread the disease?

Charles arrived before she had time to consider this point, and slid an arm around Gabrielle's slim waist, kissing her on her glowing, healthy cheek.

"Well, *ma mie?*"

She smiled at him. "We didn't expect you. There's only a stew of rabbit and vegetables."

"I could eat anything," he said with relish. "I am ravenous." He turned to Anna. "Have you introduced yourselves? *Citoyenne,* this is my half-sister, Gabrielle. Gabrielle—*Citoyenne* Anna Campbell." He pronounced her name, as always, with a strange intonation, a throttled gasp.

Gabrielle had stiffened and was staring at her. "Campbell?" she repeated. "But Charles, was that not the name of . . ."

He pushed a hand through his black hair. "Oh, yes, I forgot! This is her cousin."

The brown eyes grew cold. "And you have brought her to our house, Charles? Why?"

"They have arrested all British citizens," he said curtly. "I was summoned to her uncle—he is ill, very ill. I brought them both here. Would you have me leave them to rot in prison? Do you want the old man's death on your conscience? I do not."

Gabrielle bit her lip, shrugging. "So we give them our hospitality! My saints!" She turned and walked away very fast.

Charles looked bitterly at Anna. "I have brought a hornet's nest into my home, *citoyenne.*"

"I am very grateful to you for your generosity," she stammered, "but surely it is unwise for your family to come in contact with either myself or my uncle?"

"Your uncle has not got smallpox," he said tersely.

"What?"

"I lied to Henriot to get you both out of there—I am not sure what is wrong with him, but I suspect it is a mixture of a severe chill and the effects of shock. He will recover with careful nursing."

"Are you sure?" She was flushed with relief and hope, yet unable to quite believe the news.

"Quite sure," he nodded. "He is sleeping now. Come and eat, then you can sit with him for a few hours."

Gabrielle silently served them with large wooden bowls of stew. Anna ate slowly, afraid to let her appetite dictate her speed because her hunger was almost a physical agony. Gradually, her hunger slackened as the warmth of the stew reached her stomach. It was thick with rabbit and sliced vegetables, nourishing and full of flavor.

Charles then took her to her uncle. She saw, with distress, that Sir Henry still looked very ill.

She had somehow imagined that a few hours' sleep would improve his condition.

But his skin seemed to stretch tightly over his cheekbones, glazed and shiny with fever. There were puffy bags of bluish skin under his eyes.

"I shall have to bleed him," Charles said, after a brief examination. "You must help me."

"I?" She shrank back. She could not bear the sight of blood. But when he looked sharply at her, she forced herself to stand upright. "Yes, of course," she said huskily.

He nodded and left the room. She sat and watched Sir Henry broodingly. Charles returned with Gabrielle. They carried some instruments on a flat tray, and a jug of hot water.

Charles washed the instruments gently. His jacket was off, his shirt sleeves rolled up. Gabrielle produced a large white apron which she tied around him. He looked at her. "Heat me some wine," he said, smiling.

She smiled back. "I know!" she retorted and whisked out of the room.

Charles held out a bowl to Anna. "Hold this while I open the vein and whatever you do, don't drop it. We don't want blood all over the floor."

She winced. "If you faint I shall shake you until your head drops off," he threatened ferociously.

"I shall not faint," she said, flushing.

He studied her, then nodded. "Good."

He turned back to Sir Henry. The old man's sandy hair seemed to be glued to his head. Pink patches of skin gleamed between the damp hairs. Small veins had swollen on his nose and eyelids.

"He looks as though he is dying," she whispered in fear.

He shook his head. "He is ill, but he will not die." He picked up the evil-looking scarifier, the razor edges gleaming. His jaw was set, his cheekbones tight with determination. "I won't let him die," he said.

She turned her head aside as he set to work, holding the bowl without looking. Now and then Charles nudged the bowl into place with his elbow, but he worked in silence. At last, he muttered, "Enough!" He took the bowl from her and covered it with a cloth.

Anna stood watching her uncle anxiously, while Charles moved about the room. She heard him washing his hands. Then he lit a candle and the dusky room was mellow with a soft glow.

The shutters rattled into place. Anna looked round and saw Charles coming towards her.

"Sit down before you fall down," he said curtly.

She took a chair from the corner and brought it nearer the bed. Charles stood beside her. They both watched the sick man, who slept, but with a less hectic flush now.

Suddenly a terrible thought struck Anna. "Jeanne!" she said aloud, beginning to tremble.

"What?" Charles stared at her in bewilderment.

"My maid. She died of a fever. I may have brought the disease back to my uncle. I touched her . . ." She held out her hands, staring at them with horrorstruck eyes.

"Nonsense," he said roughly. "You cannot blame yourself! The likely answer is that he has nothing but a severe chill. Your maid's death need have nothing to do with it."

"But it could have," she sobbed. "I did not even stop to think. I went into that room!" Tears spilled down her cheeks. She was shivering.

His hands caught her shoulders. He pulled her up

into his arms, stroking her back. "Hush, you must not give in to this . . ."

She could not stop crying. Her whole body shook with sobs. His fingers moved up and touched her cheek, delicately. Her tears gushed out, soaking his shirt. Her emotion was like a storm tearing her to pieces.

"Stop it!"

His voice was harsh, and she became aware that her face was against his neck, his arm tight around her, one hand on her hair.

He pushed her away. She looked at him, quivering, her hair disheveled, her eyes shamed.

A slow, burning flush ran over her whole body.

Without a word, he walked out of the room.

Anna buried her face in her hands, hating herself. Blindly, without understanding what was happening, she had been falling in love with the last man in the world who would ever return her feelings.

Six

"My dear sir," Sir Henry exclaimed, in a feeble echo of his old impatient manner of speech, "we owe you a debt we can never repay. You do understand the penalty you may incur, I hope? Ten years, I believe, is the sentence for harboring us . . ." And he smiled wryly at Charles. "Are you sure you wish to run such a risk?"

His lean hand on the older man's wrist, Charles shook his head at him, his expression bored. "Keep still, *citoyen!* You are talking too much. You are not out of the wood, yet, you know!"

"You're a brave man, Baccoult," said Sir Henry.

"And you are a foolish one," Charles retorted, flushing slightly. "I warn you again—absolute rest is essential if you are to regain your strength."

"You have restored my faith in France," Sir Henry persisted, but fell back against his pillows in response to the doctor's menacing glare. "Well, I'll say no more, as you prefer it." He grinned. "Damnit, you have almost an Englishman's dislike of compliments."

"I had never noticed such modesty in Englishmen,"

Charles drawled, "although I have heard it remarked upon—chiefly by Englishmen."

Sir Henry laughed deeply, then coughed, his face turning dark red.

"Now, *citoyen,* are you satisfied?" Charles demanded angrily. "Is all my work to go for nothing? Sleep, sir. Sleep and no talking." He flickered a glance at Anna, seated beside the bed with some plain sewing in her lap. "And you, *citoyenne,* kindly come down and eat. You look exhausted. I do not want two patients on my hands, and while you are here, this obstinate fellow will talk to you."

She folded her sewing and rose. Sir Henry's eyes twinkled as she kissed him. As Charles left the room, her uncle whispered, "He's a choleric fellow, but a damned good doctor, and as brave a man as I've ever met. Eh, m'dear?"

"Yes, Uncle," she agreed wholeheartedly.

Charles was waiting for her outside. His black eyes shrewdly assessed her. "You have not slept for two nights. Now that your uncle is on the road to recovery I hope you will be sensible and take some rest."

"He will recover, now?" she asked eagerly.

"He'll do," Charles agreed tersely, adding, with a grin, "if he can learn to obey orders. He is not the easiest of patients."

She could not argue with that. Her first real hope had awoken when her uncle began to argue and fidget against his enforced confinement. She recognized the irritability of convalescence.

When they entered the kitchen they found Gabrielle plucking a chicken. She began scolding Charles as soon as they appeared, her voice sharply loving.

"Look at you! Worn to a thread! Sit down and get some food inside you."

He sighed wearily as he obeyed, and watched her serve him a great bowl of veal cooked in a vinous white sauce. "I am going over to Caillou this afternoon," he murmured, beginning to eat.

"Are you mad? It would be too dangerous," she exclaimed, staring at him with narrowed eyes.

He shrugged and looked up at Anna. "I have a friend in Caillou who might be prepared to take you and your uncle to England. He's a fisherman."

"A smuggler," snapped Gabrielle. "And if you are seen with him it could be disastrous for us all."

He gently touched her hand. "Give the *citoyenne* some veal, *ma mie*. She is hungry, too, you know."

Gabrielle resentfully obeyed him, slapping the meal before Anna with a toss of her head.

Anna was watching Charles with eager, doubtful eyes. "Do you really think we might get home?" Her food lay forgotten in front of her. She could not think of eating at that moment.

"It is possible," he said lightly, then nudged her with his elbow. "Eat! It is a crime to let such superb cooking go to waste."

Gabrielle flounced to her fire and began poking it vigorously. "Why do you have to get involved?" she muttered.

Charles smiled at Anna. "A doctor is regarded almost as a confessor, you know. We do not betray our patients. Once I was called to a lonely farm to take out a bullet from a smuggler's shoulder. Since then I sometimes get an anonymous gift left at my door—smuggled goods, of course, but who am I to look a gift horse in the mouth? And smugglers carry men as well as contraband."

"But the danger!" she exclaimed.

He threw her a coolly scornful glance. "No matter which route you and your uncle take out of France, *citoyenne,* you will face danger."

She flushed. "I meant the danger for you," she

stammered. "You have done too much for us already. We could not ask more of you."

Gabrielle muttered something, banging her pots about as she began to wash them.

Charles leaned back in his chair, wiping his mouth with his napkin. "What do you suggest I do with you, then? Hand you back to the Luxembourg? How do I explain my faulty diagnosis?" And when Anna did not answer, shrugged. "No, my proposal is our only hope. We will have to pay the free-traders, of course, but you can arrange that when you return to England."

"And what when the military come here asking what we have done with the foreigners?" asked Gabrielle tartly.

He grinned at her. "We show them a grave, *ma chère,* what else? It will not be the first time our churchyard has held a coffin filled with stones."

"And if they dig them up?" Gabrielle demanded furiously.

"They will not wish to dig up those who died of smallpox," he drawled. "Two British Protestants will lie quietly in our French earth for all eternity."

"How can we thank you?" Anna whispered.

"By eating your food before it is cold," he retorted, getting to his feet. He kissed Gabrielle, nodded to Anna and left the room. A few moments later she heard a horse trotting away on the dirt road.

Jean-Claud came in, wiping his face. "It is hot today," he grumbled. "Anyone would think it was high summer! Even the leaves hang on the trees as though they were waiting to be pulled off!"

"Nothing is ever good enough for you, my man," Gabrielle told him crossly, serving him his meal. "When it rains you fear a flood. When the sun shines you predict drought! You farmers are mere Jeremiahs!"

Jean-Claud began to eat, staring at Anna with open curiosity. She nervously smiled at him, wondering if he hated her as much as Gabrielle clearly did. His serious face seemed to hesitate, then he gave her a faint smile, immediately dipping his head to his food as though ashamed.

A shaggy, pointed-eared dog wandered in and came to sit between Anna and Jean-Claud. She looked down and patted his head.

"Don't touch him!" Jean-Claud barked.

She looked startled, paling. The dog turned its thin-nosed face and softly licked her hand.

"By heavens! Look at that! Did you ever see the like?" Jean-Claud gazed at her, mouth open. He turned to appeal to his sister. "Gaby, did you see that? Roland licked her!"

Gabrielle darted a bitter glance at Anna. "Like all of you the dog goes for a lady, I suppose."

Jean-Claud clicked his tongue. "Heh, Gabrielle! No call for that!"

"I'm too busy for compliments," his sister snapped, darting back and forth from larder to oven. "I have bread to make!"

"Let me help you," Anna asked nervously. "I would like to do something."

"You?" Gabrielle laughed contemptuously. "It would take twice as long if I had to teach you what to do!"

"I've made bread before," Anna claimed eagerly.

"No, thank you," the other girl said coldly.

"Oh, let her help," Jean-Claud intervened heartily. "You have often said you wished you had another female to talk to!"

"Not her, though!" Gabrielle spat, her face hard.

Anna flushed painfully, blinking back tears. "I . . . I must go and see if my uncle needs anything," she mumbled, rushing to the door.

As it closed behind her, Jean-Claud looked at his sister, reproach in his eyes. "That wasn't like you, Gaby. After all, she is not responsible for what happened to Louis. You can't blame her for what her cousin did!"

Gabrielle looked at him, face taut. "Just like a man! A pretty face and you start jumping through hoops!"

He lit a clay pipe and puffed comfortably, leaning back. "I know how you feel, *ma chère*—but be fair! The girl tries to please."

"Oh, yes," Gabrielle agreed, sneering. "She tries to please—that is what makes me suspicious of her. And you were as angry as I was yesterday. You change your tune smartly."

"Roland never makes a mistake about people," he countered stolidly. "And, anyway, Louis must be spineless to do a thing like that! A man doesn't kill himself over a girl! If every man who got jilted did that the world would soon come to an end."

"Oh, now it is Louis's fault," she mocked. "That girl certainly made an impression on you! Maybe you fancy her yourself? A poor farmer, the son of a peasant! What chance d'you think you have?"

He stood up, flushing angrily. "There's no point in talking to you in this mood! I'm off. Roland!"

The dog followed him at his command. Gabrielle patted him as he passed her and he gave a low growl. She drew back angrily.

Jean-Claud laughed loudly. "You can't kick him out of the house whenever you see him and then expect him to lick your hand," he jeered. "He knows you don't like him!"

"He's a vicious brute," she said, very red. "Get him out of my kitchen!"

Jean-Claud departed, laughing.

Charles returned next day, with a parcel of wine,

woolen cloth and some ribbons for Gabrielle, whose temper had cooled slightly over the intervening period. While she excitedly examined her present Charles told Anna that he had seen his free-trading friend. "But although he would take Sir Henry," he added soberly, "he will not take you. He is superstitious and never carries women on his fishing boat. I tried to persuade him, but he was quite adamant."

"Oh, what shall we do?" she asked despairingly.

"We could accept his terms," he suggested coolly. "Your uncle could go and I could try to get you into Switzerland. I have friends in the right circles. I think I could get traveling documents for both of us. You would have to travel under a false name, of course, but that could be arranged."

"Charles! You must be out of your head!" Gabrielle swung round on them, eyes flashing. "If you were caught it would be the guillotine!"

"Keep out of this, Gabrielle!" he ordered icily.

"No, she is right!" Anna was very pale. She pressed her hands together to stop the trembling of her fingers. "I could not allow you to run such risks for me. After all, nothing very bad would happen to me if I did return to the Luxembourg. You could say my uncle had died and I had lived."

"And when he turned up again in England?" Charles looked at Gabrielle. "Or had that point not occurred to you, *ma chère?* When Sir Henry reappears in London my little deception will be blown sky high. I shall have to get out of France with them."

"Oh, my God!" Gabrielle sank on to a stool, her face as white as her kerchief.

"We cannot accept your sacrifice," Anna said with horror. "Gabrielle and her brother will be in terrible danger."

He shook his head. "No, they will be safe enough. Gabrielle will say I isolated the two *Anglaises* and

she never even saw them. She and Jean-Claud will
know nothing except that they died and were buried.
I would not let them near the patients for fear they
caught smallpox. The story will sound plausible
enough, particularly when Gabrielle discovers I have
stolen her documents and undoubtedly used them to
smuggle the English girl out of the country. She will
be furious and scream with rage. They'll believe her."

Anna was shivering. "No, no, I could not let you
do it!"

He looked steadily at Gabrielle. "I rely on you, *ma
chère,* to put up a good performance when the military arrive. We should be out of France by then."

"Charles!" she wailed, clutching possessively at
his arm. "We would never see you again!"

"Jean-Claud will have the farm," he said quietly,
"and I do not think I can bear to go on living in
Paris much longer. You do not know what it is like.
The smell of blood fills the streets. The future looks
very black to me."

Anna lifted her chin with something of her uncle's
obstinacy. "No! It is wrong! Why should you do this
for us?"

"I do it for myself," he said curtly. "Don't argue,
citoyenne. I know what I am doing."

"Do you?" demanded Gabrielle fiercely. "Do you,
Charles? Or has your head been turned? What have
they got, these sly little *Anglaises,* that all the men of
this family run mad for them? Even Jean-Claud
pleads her case! The very dog crawls to lick her hand.
You make me sick, all of you!"

Anna was scarlet, unable to look at him.

His voice was icy as he replied, "That is enough,
Gabrielle."

The sting in his voice took effect. Gabrielle was
silent, but her eyes flashed with resentment even
while she obeyed.

"I must go and talk to Sir Henry," Charles went on in a calm voice. "He may have qualms about leaving his niece alone in France. He must consent before I put my plan into operation."

When the door had closed behind him, Gabrielle looked at Anna, her brown eyes brilliant with tears. "Are you satisfied now? You are taking him away from us forever."

"You cannot imagine that that was my intention," Anna protested indignantly, yet with compassion, since she saw that the other girl was trembling with misery and anger.

"You are the cause," Gabrielle hissed, and Anna had no defense against that charge. She could only sigh, and wish she could find the words to explain to Gabrielle all that she felt. Had she been able to dislike Gabrielle, it would have been easier to bear this hostility directed towards her. But she did like the girl. She wished she could persuade Gabrielle of the good will she felt towards anyone who was part of Charles's family.

It was always uncomfortable to be conscious of dislike of oneself. For Anna, it was doubly unpleasant because her love for Charles made her eager to please his half-sister. Had she been less shy she might have hinted at her feelings. But all she could do was bite her lip and long for the courage to speak what was in her mind.

After a silent pause, she went upstairs to her uncle, and met Charles coming down. He looked at her with a smile.

"Did my uncle agree?" she asked anxiously.

"Eventually," he nodded. "But I had a stiff, uphill task persuading him. He seemed to fear my intentions regarding you!" And the black eyes mocked her.

"I am sure he did not!" she retorted, moving towards the door. He intercepted her and their hands touched on the door knob. Hers were immediately snatched away, but she was afraid he would hear the excited beating of her heart, and drew back.

He studied her averted face. "You need not look so terrified," he drawled. "You have the air of a cornered mouse, trembling for its life. If this is what I am to expect on our journey, we shall never reach the border—you will betray us within an hour."

"I am not afraid," she stammered.

"Liar," he retorted. "You are blushing like a rose and trembling like an aspen. Are you afraid I will force my attentions upon you? You must have a pretty high opinion of me!" Dark, menacing, his face seemed to hang over her. She stared at him in confused embarrassment.

For a moment he stood there, tense as a leopard. Then he turned and continued down the stairs without another word.

Sir Henry was dozing when she entered his room. When he heard her, he jerked awake and gave her a smile. "Ah, there you are, m'dear. Baccoult has discussed this plan of his with you, I believe? Are you willing?"

"Of course, Uncle," she assured him, shaking up his pillows. He leant back against them again, watching her anxiously.

"I admit, I was against it when he first opened the idea to me, but he persuaded me that it was our best chance of escape. I still do not like the notion of leaving you behind. It does not seem right."

"We must be sensible," she assured him. "It would be more dangerous for us to travel together than apart."

He sighed gustily. "So Baccoult said. I hope he is right. I cannot avoid accepting responsibility for having brought you into this situation. I am nagged by the demons of conscience, my dear."

She recognized this last remark as his attempt at humor, and smiled. "You know I chose to remain with you. We were unfortunate, but you can hardly be held to blame for that."

The next day Charles vanished once more, to make arrangements for their escape, and Anna, having settled her uncle to sleep, went down to the kitchen to make one last effort to appease Gabrielle.

She found her in the garden, fetching water. The well lay in the center of a paved area, shaded by an old lime tree. Anna watched as Gabrielle rolled off the heavy wooden cover and let down her bucket.

Quietly Anna moved forward to operate the handle. Gabrielle looked sharply at her, but said nothing, nor did she protest when Anna helped her to carry the dripping bucket back to the house.

Pale autumn sunshine lay over the neat, even rows of vegetables, the fruit bushes and square herb garden. A patch of thin grass, shaded by gnarled apple trees, had been invaded by a flock of hens who scratched and squabbled, their toes scuffling up small clouds of dust. One of them gawkily pecked at the blowing purple heads of some daisies, then wandered away in disgust. From nearby Anna could hear the lowing of cattle and a dog barking. Roland, she guessed.

Gabrielle lowered the bucket to the kitchen floor, rolling up her sleeves to her elbows, the golden hairs on her arms glistening in the sunlight. She fitted the background perfectly, like some figure in a country landscape painted by Chardin, down to earth, glowing with health.

"I am going to do the washing," she said curtly. "You had best sit out in the sunshine while you can."

"Let me help you," said Anna, touching Gabrielle's arm pleadingly.

Gabrielle shook her head. "What could you do?"

Her scornful glance flicked Anna. "You have maids to do your work, no doubt."

"I am a poor relation," Anna protested. "I am used to helping with household duties. And I would like to help you."

Gabrielle shrugged. "Well, you could hang the clothes out later, if you insist, but I'll call you when I want you." Her tone was still brusque but less hostile, Anna thought.

She went back into the garden and sat down on a rough bench by the wall.

The leaves were falling at last, drifting down on every slight puff of wind; crisp, curled, golden as summer wine, filling the air with a restless sense of impermanence, a yearning nostalgia. The windfallen apples damply moldering under the apple trees were the haunts of wasps and flies and gave off a vinous fragrance which took her back to her childhood.

The sky was calm, blue, cloudless. But there was a bite to the air, like the cold freshness of an apple on the palate, and she shivered slightly, wishing she had a shawl to wear.

Where had Charles gone? To Paris? The very thought of the danger he must face there was enough to raise a prickle of fear along her spine. She felt helpless, maddened by her inability to do something to end the tangle which fate had made of their lives.

A leaf fluttered down beside her, the veins standing out on the transparent, skeletal leaf as though etched by acid. It had served its purpose and was discarded, but even its decay was useful; merging with the soil it would feed the roots of the tree from which it had fallen.

In her melancholy, Anna asked herself what purpose she served, what necessity dictated her existence. She felt useless. She was merely a burden to Charles, the cause of trouble to him. And she had wanted so desperately to be otherwise.

Gabrielle called her and plumped an armful of wet washing into her outstretched hands. Carefully Anna began to smooth them out over the currant bushes. Gabrielle watched her, arms akimbo, still suspicious.

Then, with a shrug, she returned to her work. They soon fell into a routine. Gabrielle did not even seem to notice when Anna joined her in the kitchen and took over the task of turning the clothes in the great tub while Gabrielle rinsed them at the stone sink. The kitchen was billowing with steam. Anna's gown was damp and stuck to her. Her cheeks were flushed, her hands wet and red. But she had evaporated her mood of melancholy, and she felt a sense of achievement in the physical release of energy.

She staggered out with Gabrielle to pour away the gray, soapy water, and laughed as they paused, afterwards, wiping their faces.

Gabrielle stared at her, then began to laugh, too. "You should see yourself! Your hair is wringing wet . . ."

"You, too!" Anna laughed, looking at Gabrielle's corn-colored hair, now darkened by water.

Gabrielle seemed to withdraw then, her face shuttered behind the old hostility. She upturned the tub and walked towards the kitchen. Anna followed, disappointed. She had felt a moment of communion with her and now it seemed to have vanished.

Gabrielle looked over her shoulder. "Coffee would be good now, eh?" Her lips moved in a faint, shy smile.

"Please," Anna responded warmly, her own face lighting up.

Gabrielle winked, lacing the coffee with brandy. "I always take a little after washing. It restores me."

When Charles returned on the following evening

he paused, in amused surprise, seeing the two girls seated over the kitchen table, absorbed in the study of each other's hands. They jumped at his greeting.

"Are you reading fortunes again, Gabrielle?" Charles demanded, grinning. "Rank superstition! You would have been burnt as a witch in the old days!"

She flushed and looked defiant. "I am often right," she claimed, then kissed him. "I am so grateful you are back safely."

He hugged her, his face kind. "And I am glad to see my own Gabrielle again."

She looked half pleased, half sheepish. "I'll make your supper," she offered, and began to beat eggs vigorously, while he sat down and smiled at Anna.

"Our arrangements are made," he said. "I've set Jean-Claud to digging a grave. I have the travel documents in my pocket, and your uncle leaves tonight."

"Tonight?" She went pale. "So soon? Will he be strong enough for the journey?"

"He must be," Charles said flatly. "It is tonight or never."

"This is like one of the Gothic romances Maria was forever reading, eh, Anna?" declared Sir Henry as they followed Charles out to the barn which lay to the west of the garden. The moon shimmered whitely over the tops of the trees. Every shadow made Anna start and tense.

The high wooden door creaked as Charles pushed it open. The shadowy interior smelt strongly of cows. Charles led the way through the animals to a ladder which led to the hay loft. Anna lifted her skirts as her feet slipped on dirty straw, and hoped that none of the cows would come too close. She had never been in such close proximity to them before and was rather nervous.

Sir Henry climbed up first, then Charles pushed Anna up, coming with her, his arm ready in case she should trip.

The loft was warm, piled high with fresh-scented, clover-rich hay in bales. Dust rose as they moved, tickling her nostrils and making her sneeze at the clouds of seed-impregnated air.

"Do not speak to each other except in very low voices," Charles warned. "I expect the curé in a moment. We are going to bury the coffins at once and I need him as a witness."

"When do I leave, m'boy?" asked Sir Henry cheerfully.

"I'll come for you as soon as the coast is clear. I'll flash my lantern and call softly. Do not move until I have flashed the lantern three times."

Sir Henry chuckled. "This is quite an adventure!"

Charles disappeared, closing the barn door behind him, and they settled down to wait. The light in the barn was dim and shifting. Pale shafts of moonlight crept through cracks in the walls and fingered the bales of hay gently, like a miser counting gold.

"You will not be too frightened, Anna, traveling across France with a stranger?" Sir Henry touched her hand reassuringly, watching her shadowy face.

She shook her head. "I trust Doctor Baccoult," she murmured unsteadily.

"Oh, indeed! A brave, good fellow!" Sir Henry was hearty and comforting, but she sensed that he was uneasy. After a pause, he went on. "I've failed you, m'dear. I blame myself. I should have left France long ago."

"You had good reasons for staying," she assured him. "Please, do not blame yourself. I do not blame you."

"Are you sincere, Anna?" He leant forward to look at her face, illumined by moonlight, and the clear width of her eyes spoke for her. He patted her hand. "You are a good girl." He lay back, sighing, against a bale of hay. "Write to me when you reach Geneva. My friend MacAndrew will arrange for your journey home to England. Give Maria my love. I hope she will not hear of our disappearance before you reach her, or the poor child will be consumed with anxiety."

Anna smiled in the concealing darkness, and promised to do all that he asked. Soon afterwards he fell into a light sleep, his head on his chest. She covered him with her shabby old cloak, and sat down again, shivering in the cold air. She thought she heard voices far off near the farmhouse, but though she listened intently she could not be certain she had really heard them.

A rustle in the hay made her jump. She turned her head and saw something move swiftly, snake-like across the floor. Rats! She shuddered, huddling herself back. The thought of their red eyes and long tails made her throat burn with nausea.

Some time later, as she hovered between sleep and waking, she heard the barn door creak open. The slow golden circle of a lantern swung in the darkness. She counted. One. Two. Three. Then Charles called softly. "Come down quickly!"

She woke her uncle. He snorted, then came to life with a jerk. "W . . . What? Eh? Oh, yes, m'dear. I'm ready."

"Ssh . . ." hissed Charles from below.

Sir Henry folded Anna's cloak around her, pressed a kiss on her temple and whispered, "Farewell, my love. Be brave. We will see each other again in England, be sure of that!"

Then he was gone and she heard the barn door creak shut once more.

She sank back, wishing she had thought to ask

Charles for a lantern. It had been hard enough to watch the rats scampering past her while her uncle had been within call. Now that she was alone she did not know how she would bear it.

She moved nearer the edge of the loft, her eyes fixed on the barn door. The sight of it gave her courage. Below, the cows moved from time to time, tails flicking, champing, the stale odor of their hides rising to her nostrils. Once she might have found the strong scent distasteful, but now she found it comforting: an animal warmth that helped her to forget the furtive, alien scurrying of the rats.

Very slowly, the pale light of dawn crept in through cracks in the walls, forming little patches and colonies of gray among the shadows, which spread gradually, until the whole barn was full of light.

The cows grew restless. They tossed their heads and lowed, knowing that it was time for milking, time to be led out to the fields to eat the crisp stubble left from harvest.

She, too, waited, hopefully, for Jean-Claud's arrival. Her hands and feet were numb, she was stiff and chilled, and thought eagerly of a cup of hot coffee.

When she heard the sound of feet approaching, she stood up to brush her gown free of wisps of hay.

The barn door was pushed open. Anna glanced round her bale of hay, wondering if it was Charles or Jean-Claud.

Then her heart thudded painfully. It was neither. The intruder was a French soldier, his musket presented into the barn, his face alert and suspicious.

Seven

His gaze wandered around, over the rippling backs of the cows, the flies which were beginning to buzz in the straw, the farm implements hanging on the walls.

Then he glanced upward. Anna froze on the spot, hoping he would not see her behind her bale of hay.

She heard his feet scuffle in the straw as he moved forward. Her breath had been held so long it was beginning to hurt.

Then she saw something that made her almost faint with terror. The sunlight, sliding over the loft, had outlined her shadow on the wall. She pressed in close to the bale of hay, but the shadow was still recognizably that of a woman.

"Ah, there you are, *citoyen soldat!*" Gabrielle's voice was bright and cheerful. "Do you want some coffee? Better hurry or the corporal will drink it all."

Nervously Anna peered round her bale. She saw Gabrielle in the barn doorway, smiling flirtatiously, her hair like gold in the sunlight. The soldier lowered his musket.

"You have fine fat cows, *citoyenne*. Come and show me your barn."

"I know you soldiers," Gabrielle retorted, with a toss of her head. "You just want a kiss in the straw! Do you want to get me into trouble?" And she skipped away, smiling invitingly over her shoulder.

The soldier laughed. "I'll catch you, my pretty!" The door slammed. The rickety walls shivered. The silvery sound of Gabrielle's laughter came floating back. Then silence.

There were doves roosting up in the beams. Their bright eyes and white wings flashed by on beams of sunlight, swooping in and out of an opening high up in the roof. Jean-Claud came in and drove out the cows, never glancing up at the loft. She longed to ask him what was happening, but dared make no sign.

She was not sure how long it was before Charles came for her. She was half asleep, her head on the hay, drowsily drifting in a beautiful dream of him, when his voice brought her back to reality.

"They have gone! You can come down now!"

He helped her down the ladder, holding her waist. Her limbs trembled at the unaccustomed movement after so long a period of keeping very still. He held her, looking down at her face.

"My uncle? He got away safely?"

"He will be on board the fishing boat by now," Charles assured her.

"Why were soldiers here?"

"They were local men," he said easily. "Just a routine visit. I reported the death of my two patients to the local committee. They sent some men to check. They spent most of the time in the kitchen. Gabrielle plied them with wine and they went off very cheerfully."

"Did they seem convinced?" She looked up at him

anxiously. He seemed rather pale. She wondered if he had been nervous during the search.

"They saw me burning the bedding from the room you had supposedly died in—I think they were convinced. They did not search the upper floor. Afraid of catching smallpox, probably. I asked Sir Henry to keep his story secret for as long as possible, to give us a chance to get out of France before the authorities realize what has happened."

"I am worried about Gabrielle and Jean-Claud," she said uneasily. "I do not want them to suffer for me."

"They will not," he assured her. "I told you—, their story will be believed. After all, the soldiers who came here would not go into that room, so why should anyone else? Only I knew. Only I arranged it."

They went back to the farmhouse and ate the meal Gabrielle had ready. Jean-Claud and Roland came into the kitchen, and the dog crept to Anna and put his head on her lap. As always, Jean-Claud grinned and seemed pleased by this evidence of affection.

"Get that dirty animal out of my kitchen," snapped Gabrielle, very flushed from baking.

"He's no dirtier than I am," claimed Jean-Claud stubbornly.

"And you can wash yourself, too," his sister told him.

Anna fondled Roland's ear. The dog licked her hand, gazing at her out of large, brown, liquid eyes.

"Ugh, how can you bear to touch him?" said Gabrielle. "He's alive with fleas."

"Poor boy," Anna murmured, scratching Roland under his chin.

The sympathy in her voice made him fawn on her delightedly, tail wagging from side to side.

When they were ready to set out on their journey, Charles hugged Gabrielle, who was openly weeping. "Cheer up! This trouble cannot last forever. I will come back to France one day."

"But when?" she wailed.

Jean-Claud pulled her hand, smiling at Charles over her head. "Heh, Gabrielle! Charles must be off or it will be too late!"

Anna looked at Gabrielle, hesitating, doubting. Gabrielle looked back, her lip trembling. Then she muttered, "Well, *Anglaise,* good luck!" And smiled waveringly.

Anna impulsively kissed her. "Thank you," she whispered. "And I am sorry. I really am sorry."

They were to take the coach from a crossroads a kilometer and a half away. They had to walk there, carrying the two small valises packed with anonymous clothing, and Anna was glad it was not raining.

She looked back once, wistfully, at the timbered house set so snugly among encircling trees. It seemed a long time since she had had her first sight of it. It was like walking out of security into a world full of danger. Ahead of them lay who knew what traps.

The day was windy and sunless. The wind had risen overnight and stripped the last leaves. They walked through oceans of them, their feet crackling as though they walked over sugar.

They passed between tall oaks, their branches bare, the ground around them littered with acorns. A herd of pigs were grazing underneath and seated on a fallen tree an old man in tattered clothes was eating some bread. He looked up and stared at the two travelers. Charles nodded to him and called a polite greeting. The old man replied mumblingly, his gaze wary.

They waited at the crossroads a full half hour. Charles stood tensely staring around at the empty countryside. Harvesting was over. There was no human being in sight anywhere.

At last the rolling cloud of dust told them that the coach was coming. Charles hailed it and spoke to the driver, who spat on the ground, grunting, as though unwilling to take them up. But at last he nodded, and Charles pushed Anna aboard, paid their fares and climbed up himself.

The coach was half empty. The other passengers stared at the new arrivals. An old woman with a basket on her knees offered to move up to make room for Anna in the corner.

"I dare say you would prefer to look out of the window," she smiled. "It makes me giddy to see how the world rushes by—but you young things are used to it!"

Anna heard a faint mewing from the basket. Gratefully accepting the offered corner seat, she asked if the old woman had a cat with her, and was shown the curled-up, fluffy little kitten, lying on a piece of flannel in the basket.

"He's a good little fellow. He hardly stirs. See, he is quite sleepy. I put a wee drop of brandy in his milk before we set out and it has made him so contented!"

"He is very pretty!" Anna said, smiling.

The old woman looked pleased. "Where are you bound for, *citoyenne?*"

"Dijon," Anna answered casually.

"You are not from Dijon, I'll be bound," the old woman nodded.

Anna felt Charles tense. Their eyes met across the coach. "No," she replied, keeping her voice level. "How did you guess that, *citoyenne?*" Never had she been so grateful for her fluent French. The other two passengers were staring at her and she felt very nervous.

"That is a Parisian accent," the old woman said triumphantly, looking around for applause.

"Quite right!" Anna laughed, a trifle too loudly, and her eyes met Charles's again, with relief.

A red-faced farmer was seated opposite Charles. He mournfully surveyed the landscape as they rattled along. "Poor harvest again," he grunted to Charles. "Very poor."

Charles replied in the local patois he had always used to Gabrielle, "We had such a rainy summer!"

"Rain?" The farmer heaved himself up. "It came down in buckets day after day! We would have done better to plant rice!"

Charles laughed at this old farmer's joke, which he had heard so many times before.

Anna, glancing round from the window, caught the third passenger staring at her, and flushed slightly.

He was a small, sharp-featured man in black, with thin lips and narrow, lashless eyes of an indeterminate color. He leaned back, arms folded, his glance moving from Anna to Charles.

Anna turned back to her contemplation of the landscape, but something had stirred in her mind. There was something vaguely familiar about the little man. She was sure she had seen him before, and alarm bells rang violently.

Where was it? If he should recognize her, it could be quite disastrous. But he made no sign of recognition. He seemed to be mildly curious about her, it was true, but surely if he had any idea of her identity he would have said something.

She turned her head, as though casually, and let her eyes drift past him. A sigh of relief caught her as she saw that he was now, apparently, sleeping, his head slumped forward on his chest, the strange eyes closed.

But although her immediate fear was removed, the

vague memory kept nudging at her. Several times she thought she remembered, but the memory sank back again before she could quite capture it.

The more she thought about it, the less certain she became. He was such a very easy person to pass over. Silent, pale, without any distinguishing feature. Yet every time her eye touched him she felt again that nudge, that fleeting conviction of recognition.

As mile after mile rumbled past all the passengers fell into uneasy dozes. Anna slept with her head against the window, her body curled against the seat.

They stopped at a small country *auberge* for a meal, while the horses were fed and watered. Charles and Anna were ushered into a quiet parlor, the old woman vanished away into the night with her basket and the farmer pushed his way into the crowded bar for a drink of good red wine.

The landlord came to take Charles's order, slapping at the dirty table with his apron in an apologetic manner. "What will you have, *citoyen*? Game pie? Veal?"

Charles ordered the veal and a bottle of local white wine. When they were alone again, he glanced at Anna. "What is it? You have been staring at nothing with a frown on your face ever since we got here. Is something troubling you?"

She hesitated. She did not want to alarm him, but she had to confide her anxiety to him before it choked her.

"The little man, on the coach," she said quietly, bending towards him for fear of eavesdroppers.

Charles shot her an acute glance. "What of him?"

"I may be wrong, but I have the feeling I have seen him before."

Charles looked disturbed. "Where?"

"I cannot remember. It has been worrying me ever since we got on the coach. I am sure I have met him, but I do not know if he remembers me. There was something about the way he looked at me that made me suspect he did—but, again, I cannot be certain. It is just a feeling."

Charles put his elbows on the table and stared at her, his brows drawn together. "Try to think where you could have met him," he urged. "He looks like a Parisian to me. That ferrety face does not fit the country landscape."

She nodded. "Perhaps if I heard him speak I should recognize him, but he said nothing on the coach."

Charles nodded. "Where is he now, I wonder? Did you notice what he did when we got down from the coach?"

"I did see him in the stable yard," she admitted, "but it was so dark out there—I do not know what he did after that."

"I wonder if he joined our farmer friend in the bar," Charles said thoughtfully. He pushed back his chair and stood up. "Stay here, Anna. I am going to take a look."

She looked nervously after him, her hands trembling. The landlord arrived while he was gone and stared at his chair in suspicious surprise.

"My companion will be back shortly," stammered Anna. "He . . . he forgot something."

The landlord gave her a wink, setting the table deftly, giving the spoons a final polish with his apron. "Aye, *citoyenne*," he murmured. "No need to be embarrassed. Nature calls us all!"

Anna blushed as the door closed behind him.

A few moments later Charles returned and gave her a smile of reassurance. "As I hoped, our ferrety friend is drinking with the farmer. Let us trust he does not remember you. Perhaps, like yourself, he has a faint recollection, but cannot pin it down."

The meal was excellent, and the wine relaxed Anna's nerves until she felt almost confident of their eventual success. When they returned to the coach she was warm, full and sleepy.

The farmer and the black-coated stranger were late in arriving, and seemed very merry. Their voices could be heard upraised in song before they were in sight.

Charles was sitting opposite Anna, in the other corner seat. The farmer stumbled, as he climbed aboard, to the querulous complaints of the driver, and fell across Charles, laughing foolishly.

"Beg pardon, *citoyen*, I'm sure," he apologized cheerfully, and settled down beside Charles, his face even more violently red than before. An aroma of wine and brandy floated around him. He fell at once into a heavy, snoring sleep.

His companion stepped up lightly and took his place beside Anna. His face was as pale as ever, his eyes as sharp and alert, before his thick lids fell and veiled them.

Charles watched him from behind his hat, which he had drawn down low over his brow.

Out of his greatcoat pocket the black-coated stranger drew a bottle of brandy, which he offered to Charles.

"You are most kind, *citoyen*," Charles responded. He drank politely and handed it back, with a patriotic sentiment. "Death to the enemies of France!"

The indeterminate eyes narrowed on him. The stranger smiled. "Indeed," he murmured, swallowing a mouthful of brandy.

Anna was baffled as Charles, very jovial, launched a conversation with the other man. But then it occurred to her that he was trying to persuade the man to talk so that she might remember his voice.

"You are making a long journey, *citoyen?*" Charles asked, smiling broadly.

The little man spread his hands. "That depends," he murmured. His voice was light, thready. Anna listened desperately, but it rang no bells. She could not recall having heard it before.

"Depends upon what?" Charles asked, still very friendly.

The other man glanced carefully at the snoring farmer. His light voice murmured, "Upon you, *citoyen.*"

Charles sat upright, tensed and wary. "On me?" He laughed loudly. "What the devil does that mean?"

"How much money do you carry on you, *citoyen?*" The light voice was still courteous, yet there was a steely thread running beneath it that warned the two listeners that the time for humor had gone.

Charles leaned back, casual and relaxed, but Anna saw that his black eyes were narrowed and hard.

"What is that to you?" he demanded.

"I am a commissary of the people's republic," the other replied coolly. "A short time ago I was on duty in our committee rooms when a party of English prisoners were brought in . . ." He glanced down, sideways, at Anna, his thin brows raised. "There were few women among them. I might not, perhaps, have recognized one of the men. But I noticed all the women."

Anna's heart seemed to flip over and fall a long way. She looked despairingly at Charles. He was still leaning back, his hands thrust into his pockets, watching the little man with a thoughtful expression.

"And so, *citoyen?*" he demanded coolly.

The other man shrugged. "Three days ago I heard that my brother was dying. He has eight children, five of them girls. Pretty little creatures, I am very fond of them. But I am a poor man, *citoyen.* I could not provide for so many children without ruining myself."

"A sad tale, *citoyen*," Charles replied politely. "You have my deepest sympathy."

"You are very kind." The thin mouth straightened. "Money is worthless to the dead, they say, but the living need it badly."

Their eyes met. Charles stared hard, his black eyes narrowed. The pale, indeterminate eyes were steady and unrelenting in return.

Charles nodded slowly. "We have a long journey ahead of us. We need most of the money I carry with me." He pulled out his pocket book, stuffed with paper money. "The value of our money falls so often that I barely have enough."

The other man reached over and took the money. Anna watched, uneasily, as he counted it on the seat. He separated it into two piles, one large, one small.

"What is a life worth, anyway?" he murmured, as though to himself. "I would give all I have to save my brother's life." He looked at Charles. "What do you think, *citoyen?* If it saves a life does money matter?"

Charles took off his hat and thrust his fingers through his curly black hair. Then he grimaced, leant forward and picked up the smaller pile.

Almost like a conjuring trick, the little man had snatched up the other pile and pushed it into his pocket, so fast that Anna hardly saw it happen.

He settled back, without a word, his hat over his eyes, and soon was snoring gently.

They stopped at a village inn to take up a nervous old man who clutched his traveling bag on his knee and eyed them all suspiciously. When the coach moved on Anna suddenly realized that the gentle-

man in black had vanished in the confusion of the
halt. She had not even noticed.

Across the coach her eyes met those of Charles.
He rapped on the trap door in the roof and spoke to
the coachman. A few moments later the coach rumbled to a stop and Charles helped Anna down.

They watched the rear lamps of the coach vanish.
Anna looked up at Charles. "Where are we? Why
have we stopped here?"

"We had paid our fares to the next town," he
told her. "We were to spend the night there. If our
blackmailing friend intends to set the military after
us that is where they will search for us. As we are
now desperately in need of money, we would have
to a make a detour anyway, so I decided to pay a
visit to an old friend of mine who lives in these
parts."

He took her arm. "It is a long walk across country. Do you feel you can keep up with me?"

"Oh, yes," she agreed eagerly, falling into step.
The road was rutted and muddy, covered with drifting leaves which had blown into heaps, and rustled
beneath their feet. Poplar trees lined the banks on
either side. The rising moon glided up behind the
whispering branches and hung, a pale visitor, staring at them.

Charles halted after a few moments, and stared
around. Then he helped Anna climb the bank and
they threaded their way round the outskirts of a vine-
yard, descending into a sunken lane on the far side,
and walking briskly to the east. Branches creaked
eerily above their heads. An owl swished out of the
trees, its eyes yellow as lamps, and a second or two
later came the high keening of a small animal caught
by fierce talons.

Anna gave a little cry of dismay. There had been
so much pitiful despair in the sound. Charles looked

down, his face a shadowy oval under his hat. His arm pressed her hand against his side.

"Nature is cruel," he said softly.

"I had forgotten how cruel," she answered. "When I was a child I often saw such things. In London and Paris it was only man who seemed cruel, but in reality the whole world is full of savage cruelty."

Charles laughed. "That is moving to the other extreme. No, we have to recognize that there is cruelty, but it is balanced by finer things. Civilization is the result of that balance: when man's natural savagery is checked by his natural generosity."

The lane ran sharply downhill. At the bottom Anna could see the huddled shapes of some small cottages. Charles whispered to her to be absolutely silent. They passed behind the cottages, walking very carefully.

The crack of a twig under her feet made Anna's heart thud. She stopped dead, listening. Charles tugged at her arm and they walked on, but she was trembling.

Charles slowly, silently pushed open a wicket gate, and they moved up a long path, under the grabbing branches of some thorn bushes.

Charles stood staring at the house to which they had come. The windows were all dark and shuttered. He tapped softly on the kitchen door. Nothing stirred, but the wind, rattling the leaves along the path behind them, made Anna start and turn, her hands at her breast.

Charles picked up some loose stones and threw them at the bedroom window above them. They rattled and fell back. There was a pause. Charles threw some more, taking careful aim.

After another moment, the shutters were pushed back and a voice demanded crossly to know what was the matter.

"Henri! It is me, Charles!"

A silence. Then, "Charles? *Sacre bleu* . . . Charles, do you say? What the devil . . . but wait! I am coming. I am coming down . . ."

The window shut. A thin shaft of light came from the room, then vanished.

A few moments later the door opened. A man held up a flickering candle and studied them.

Anna's breath was taken away by the sheer magnificence of his size. He loomed over them like Goliath over David, a loose robe flowing around him as the sea flows around a rock.

"Charles! It really is you! *Ma foi,* I thought I was having a hallucination. I have been drinking to-night and I was expecting to see a few strange things. But, come in, don't stand out there in the night air—come in!"

He moved back, the candle held high, and bowed as Anna passed him. She found herself in a small kitchen, cluttered and untidy, smelling strongly of wine.

She heard the bolts ram home on the door. The giant put his candle on the table and turned to embrace Charles warmly, his enormous hands clapping him on the back.

He made Charles look like a reed beside the enormous girth and magnitude of his own build. His fierce red hair bristled in rough tufts, uncombed and tangled. His eyes were as green and round as glass beads. His nose was huge and bulbous, the nostrils flared like those of a horse.

"You scabrous young devil!" he bellowed. "What are you doing out here in the back of beyond? I thought you were in Paris. Are you fleeing from Madame la Guillotine?" His voice seemed to rebound from the walls of his chest, deep and booming, like the echo in a cavern.

"Softly, Henri, softly!" Charles grinned. "You have put our case in a nutshell, but let us keep it within these four walls."

The big man drew back, staring at him. "Holy Shroud, I was joking! Are you really in trouble, Charles?"

Charles drew an explicit finger over his throat, nodding.

The big man whistled, his green eyes very round. "That's bad! But," he cheered up, "we will get you out of it! Never fear!"

Charles drew Anna forward. "Anna, may I present my very dear friend, Doctor Henri Lasceux? Henri, this is Anna. She is traveling on Gabrielle's documents, so try to remember that she is using the name Gabrielle Petellat—in case you should be asked."

Doctor Lasceux bent his bulk to kiss Anna's hand, his green eyes probing her face.

"She's pale. I prescribe eight hours' sleep," he rumbled.

"I am not tired," said Anna. She had no intention of being packed off to bed.

"She is English," Charles drawled, looking mockingly at her. "And, of course, like all that nation, stubborn as a mule."

His friend roared. He rolled around the kitchen fishing food and drink out of the confusion on the shelves. Soon the table was spread with bread, cheese, wine, and they were seated around it, the candlelight carving their faces into strange, angular shapes.

"Who else is in the cottage?" asked Charles, cutting himself a large chunk of cheese.

"Just myself," said Henri. "My wife is staying with her sister, who is delivering herself of an eleventh child. We have a maid who comes in every morning to do the heavy work, but she sleeps at home. So tell me your tale freely. *J'aime les contes,* you know. I love being told stories even at night, when I have a hangover." And his grass-green eyes winked at Anna.

She smiled back. She felt drawn to the big, smiling giant, whose green eyes were at the same time shrewd and sharp, and as gentle as a woman's.

Pouring himself a glass of wine, Charles rapidly unfolded their story, beginning from Anna's arrest and ending with the encounter with the gentleman in black.

"The sneaking little rat!" exploded Henri, his vast hand slamming down on the table, making everything on it rattle. "I would have slit his gizzard for him before I had given him a sou!"

"I had to think of Anna," Charles shrugged. "And if he does hold his tongue we will have bought wisely. Of course, he may have taken our money and still intended to inform on us. Who can tell? He looked capable of it."

Henri ground his teeth, his green eyes flashing. Then his laughter rumbled in his chest again. "But to bury two coffins full of stones! What a joke! I wish I had thought of that! You're an ingenious rascal, Charles. How they will curse when they dig them up —I wish I could be there to see it! I love to see these petty bureaucrats knocked into the mud."

Charles grinned. "I have a suspicion that they will ignore the whole episode. They hate to look fools, and to dig the coffins up would set the whole of Paris laughing at them."

Henri bellowed with laughter. "Aye, true. Those tinpot tyrants fear laughter more than the plague." He leaned back, making his chair creak protestingly. "But you need money, my friend. I'm not a rich man, but I have a few sous upstairs. I live very simply. I have no need for much money. You are welcome to what I have, you know that. There should be more than enough to get you to Switzerland."

Charles leaned across and embraced him. "I relied on you, Henri—I knew you would help if you could! Thank you."

The other man pushed away his gratitude with a grin. "It is nothing! Now, I have a pony cart that will take you to Eaux-de-Sainte-Marie—it is six miles off and would be too far for the young lady to walk. A coach calls there at noon twice a week. It will call tomorrow."

Charles thanked him again. "That will help to throw them off the track. They will not look for us so far afield."

"That is what I thought," agreed Henri. "Leave my cart with the landlord of the Three Golden Cocks. He's a close-mouthed fellow who owes me a favor. You may trust him. The coach stops there. But be careful of the ostlers. They are a miserable, sneaking crew. Keep out of their way if you can."

He looked down kindly at Anna, whose head was slipping towards her chest. "The little *citoyenne* is weary, my friend. I suggest we all retire now."

Anna slept deeply, her mind troubled by occasional fleeting nightmares, but warm as toast in the great feather bed, with a heavy patchwork quilt flung over her.

By daylight the kitchen seemed a cheerful place. A marmalade cat sat cleaning its paws on the window sill, among a row of pots of geraniums, and the smell of coffee pervaded everywhere.

Anna's spirits rose as she ate her breakfast. Henri crammed food into his mouth, chewing with gusto, his vast frame forced into a dark green jacket and biscuit breeches.

"Are your documents water-tight?" he asked Charles.

"They will pass, I hope," Charles said, frowning. "They are all I could manage. I borrowed Gabrielle's papers to get Anna a traveling pass. We must hope that none of the border guards are too inquisitive."

"You know," Henri said, glancing mischievously from one to the other, "there is one certain way of passing unscathed through the border."

"What's that?" asked Charles, his face indulgent, expecting one of Henri's high-flown jokes.

"You could marry the girl!"

Eight

Anna put down her cup so suddenly that hot liquid spilled over her hand and ran down on to her skirt.

"I'm sorry," she stammered, cheeks burning. She stared down at the spreading stain on her gown with eyes that barely focused.

Henri chuckled. "It is I who should apologize, young lady—I startled you." He gave Charles a wicked grin, shifting in his seat so that the chair groaned under his weight.

Anna jumped up. Dipping a handkerchief in the water bucket which stood in a corner, she began to rub at the coffee stain.

"You are silent, *mon ami,*" Henri murmured to Charles. "Do you not think my idea an excellent one? Who would suspect a husband and wife?"

Anna could not help turning to look at Charles. He was watching her, his face impassive.

Slowly, he said, "It would solve one problem, of course."

Anna gasped. "No! I could not!" The violence of her exclamation made Charles raise his brows. For a second there was something in his own face that startled her.

Henri was looking from one to the other of them; amused, mischievous, watchful.

"My friend Guibert, the notary at Eaux-de-Sainte-Marie, could arrange everything for you," he said. "Guibert is very discreet."

"We would need more than discretion," Charles said. "We would need the devil's own luck."

The very idea of marrying Charles without love would be a mockery of all her deepest feelings. Anna turned, suddenly, and ran out into the sunny garden. She stumbled and caught at a tree, staring unseeingly over the untidy tangle of bushes, trees and weeds. Birds flew up in a panic and perched in remote branches, peering down at her.

Charles came up behind her and caught her by the shoulder, pulling her round to face him.

"You need not be in such a quake, *citoyenne*. I have not the slightest intention of forcing you into a loveless marriage."

"You sounded as though you were taking it seriously . . ."

"Did I? Perhaps I was refusing to allow Henri to tease me into the sort of display you indulged in . . ." His voice was scathing.

Rigid with anger, she flung back, "Did you enjoy making me look a fool?"

"You did that yourself. Your face was a picture . . . panic gave you a witless look for a while."

"How dare you?" Her voice soared, sharp with anger and pain, and her hand flew up to strike him, involuntarily.

He caught her wrist before she had finished the action, held her poised, his eyes narrowed on her flushed, furious face.

"I did not think you had such spirit! What has

made you so belligerent? The idea of finding yourself shackled to one of the lower classes? There is
nothing like self-interest for arousing passion, is
there?"

"When I marry I want it to mean something, to
be beautiful, not to be a cheap trick which I could
only remember with shame."

"You would remember it as the day you saved
your skin at the expense of a few principles," he
said sarcastically.

"I would rather go back to the Luxembourg!"

His lip curled. "And take me with you? I suppose,
when we met on the tumbrils you would apologize
sweetly for your slight error of judgment, and expect
my forgiveness?"

She looked at him despairingly. She might risk her
own life. How could she throw his away lightly?

"You said . . . you said you were not thinking of
it . . ." she whispered.

"My reasons are more honest than yours," he said,
the handsome dark face taut with disgust and anger.

"Your reasons? What are they?"

He moved away from her and stared up at the sky.
"Sound, sensible reasons. We dare not approach the
authorities unless we have no choice . . . it would be
too dangerous for us to try to marry. That was what I
meant when I said it would solve one problem. I
was going to continue by pointing out how many
more it would create. We shall have to avoid contact
with officialdom in all its forms. It would be sheer
folly to marry, in fact."

She swallowed. "Oh."

He swung to look at her, his eyes contemptuous.
"Oh, indeed. You could have saved yourself your
little flurry of horror at the idea of marriage to me."

"I . . ." The words of denial stuck in her throat.
How could she admit to him he was mistaken, with-

out revealing more of her feelings than she could bear to have him guess?

He walked back towards the house. She followed, wishing frantically that she had not made such a mess of things. Lately, they had seemed to be on better terms. His bitter antagonism had seemed to grow less. Suddenly, it was all back again. The name of his brother lay between them, unspoken, yet potent. He thought that she had fled from the very thought of marriage with him for the same contemptible reasons which had made Maria reject Louis so cruelly.

Henri grinned at them. "Is it settled? I did not think I would ever act as Cupid to you, my friend. It is a role somewhat unsuited to my figure!"

"The idea was clever, but impractical," Charles said carefully. "My dear Henri, think of the danger we would run! Our papers would not stand up to any careful scrutiny. It would be madness to venture near an official."

Henri scratched his chin. "I see what you mean! A pity! It seemed a romantic notion."

Charles shot Anna a glance of sardonic mockery. "Oh, highly romantic," he murmured.

She moved uneasily, averting her gaze.

"The *citoyenne*, however, did not think so—the English have no sense of humor." Charles used a voice as smooth as silk, but the sting hidden beneath the words penetrated, and Anna bit her lip.

They left for Eaux-de-Sainte-Marie shortly afterwards, driving at a rattling pace behind a fat pony which, while avoiding the worst of the ruts for itself, was apparently determined to throw them all into a ditch if it could manage to do so, so that Anna was forced to clutch at Charles from time to time.

At length he slid an arm about her, glancing down into her face with such a sardonic expression that she could willingly have hit him.

"So, I am useful for some things?" he murmured under his breath.

The sky was tinted a pale lavender. A wind had arisen, blowing fallen leaves into Anna's lap and tossing her hair into wild confusion. The sun was not visible. The air was chilly, and the bare trees had a wintry look against the livid sky.

"A storm blowing up," Henri commented. He leaned forward, and the little cart tilted perilously. Forgetting her dignity, Anna clung to Charles.

It infuriated her to see him grin. Between the lids, lowered over his black eyes, she caught a dark, ironic gleam.

They approached the little country town by a back route which led directly to the Three Golden Cocks. A surly ostler strolled out reluctantly to take the pony's head.

He nodded to Henri, stared curiously at the two strangers.

"Shall I stable her?" he asked Henri.

"Yes, *mon brave,*" Henri retorted. The ostler looked even more sullen, but began to lead the pony away.

Watching him, Anna caught a strange backward glance, felt a quiver of alarm. Was it her imagination, or had there been a gleam of sly suspicion in those eyes?

Out of the inn came a cheerful, loud-voiced land-lord, who greeted Henri warmly.

"What luck! Today of all days, Henri, for you to come into town! My mother-in-law, poor old bag of bones, has fallen down the stairs and broken her leg. Will you go round and see to it? I would have got Roger, but he drank two bottles of brandy last night and is as sick as a dog this morning!"

Henri chuckled. "Ah, my poor Roger! He never learns, does he? I might have known that if I came to town I would find him in one of his bad times. What was it? That nag of a wife of his?"

The landlord shrugged. "What else?" He glanced at Charles and Anna.

"This is my very dear old friend Charles Baccoult, whom I have known since we were young! He and his sister are here to take the *diligence* for Dijon," Henri said.

The landlord greeted them politely. "So," he said, "this is what brought you here, Henri! The *diligence* should be here any moment."

"Then I will wait to see you safely aboard," Henri told them.

The landlord gestured. "Come into the kitchen and take a glass of something with me—it is a cold day."

They followed him into a large, dark kitchen. A plump woman was stirring a pot over a fire. A cat lay beneath a large table, staring with fixed eyes into a corner, the tip of her tail twitching, Anna thought she saw a slight movement there. Mice, she decided, shrugging.

They each had a glass of red wine. The woman watched them, unspeaking yet not unfriendly.

They heard the sound of the wheels grating over the yard a few moments later. Henri embraced them, winked, followed them out to see them aboard.

The driver solemnly inspected their papers, then handed them back. Anna looked at Charles, biting her lip. She had to look away. Charles, too, had seen the driver read their documents upside down. A sigh of mixed relief and amusement shook her. If only such luck could follow them all the way!

They waved farewell to Henri, who stood in the center of the yard as they moved off, an enormous, billowing figure, his cloak blowing in the wind, his hat swinging round and round over his head in a jovial salute.

Anna caught a look on Charles's face; read hurt and regret in his black eyes. When would he ever see Henri again, she wondered. It made her ashamed to think how much Charles was losing. But for her he would be safe in Paris, a respected doctor. Ahead of him lay exile, poverty, loneliness. And it was all her fault.

She looked at the other passengers, remembering with fresh anxiety how far they yet had to go before they reached safety. Two thin, black-garbed women, clutching baskets, looked curiously back at her. They were probably sisters, she decided, seeing the resemblance between them. Beside Charles sat a sturdy, well-dressed man with a wary expression. From his dress he was in some profitable way of business. He caught her eye, looked away quickly. There was one other young man, much younger than Charles, with curly brown hair, trimmed fashionably, and bright blue eyes. He smiled as she glanced at him. She smiled in return, then blushed as she saw the admiration in his eyes.

The coach rumbled on, under the stormy sky, with the wind occasionally roaring down on them and making the coach sway perilously.

Thunder growled suddenly, and then the dark sky split with a lightning flash much nearer.

Charles leant forward, his hand touching her lightly.

"We are quite safe in a moving vehicle," he told her with gentle reassurance.

She blushed, seeing all eyes turned on her. The two older women nodded their agreement.

"Oh, everyone knows that, *citoyenne!*"

The coach swayed violently, taking a corner, throwing Anna against the curly-headed young man, who supported her quickly, his arm sliding round her.

Charles looked across at him coolly, eyes hard, and as Anna looked at him, frowned in warning. She knew he was reminding her that she must not get into conversation if she could avoid it. The less attention they attracted the better. She might betray them by an unguarded word.

The young man, intercepting the exchanged glances, clearly felt uncomfortable and hurriedly released her, flushing, uncertain as to their relationship.

Anna closed her eyes. The best plan was to pretend sleep. At least, then, she could make no mistakes.

From a pretense she gradually slipped into reality, her head drooping down on to her chest. Far away the storm seemed to drift, like the sound of distant gunfire, and she dreamed of Paris; of angry mobs in the streets and alleys, of menace and suspicion everywhere, like a shadowy fog, in which figures loom and vanish without reason.

She was awoken by a grinding sound, and fell heavily forward. Charles caught her and she felt his arms, hard, around her, heard his breathing close to her ears in the darkness that now surrounded them.

The coach was tilted forward at an angle. The other passengers had all fallen sideways when she fell. They all began to right themselves.

The other women were alarmed. "What has happened? What is it? Robbers! We have been held up!"

Charles stuck his head out of the window and shouted. "What's wrong?"

"A tree down in the road. We ran right into it! Well, how could I see in the dark? One of the wheels has come off . . . we're half in a ditch! Everybody out before she sinks further into the mud . . ."

The coachman had appeared, was opening the door and gesturing sullenly to them.

"It is pouring out there! We will be soaked to the

skin!" The thin women began to complain, to protest.

"Can I help it? Even the lantern is shattered!" The driver glared at them.

Charles jumped down, turned to help Anna. She felt his hands tighten on her waist. His eyes flashed at her in the darkness. The road was awash with muddy water. Charles put a hand beneath her arm.

The coachman had moved away. Morosely, his greatcoat collar turned up against the steadily falling rain, he was kicking the broken wheel.

"I have already sent my guard down the road," he told them. "There's a wheelwright at Pont-St. Jean, but can't say whether he will come out on a night like this! You would be wise to walk on there and take a room for the night."

"How far is this village?"

"Not far—ten minutes' walk. I should hurry. First come, first served. They will all want rooms."

Charles took her arm, urged her forward. In this pitch darkness, on a wet, rutted road, it was hard going, and her skirts were soon sodden, clinging to her legs, making her shiver.

Trees hung over the road. From somewhere in their upper branches she caught a flash of white, then something swooped down, making a weird sound as it passed.

She gasped in panic, turned and clung to Charles, shuddering. His arms closed round her.

"Only an owl!" he whispered.

She gulped, drew away, still shivering. "I . . . I am sorry. I must be on edge . . ."

He looked down at her, still holding her. For a second their eyes held. She could see only the shining of his glance. His face was shadowed.

He bent his head too swiftly for her to anticipate him. His mouth took hard possession of her lips, parting them, warm and human against the responsive quiver she involuntarily gave. His hands tightened on her waist briefly, which was as well, for her legs appeared to have turned to water and she had to clutch at him to stay upright.

Then, behind them, they heard voices. The other passengers were hard on their heels. Charles released her. They walked in silence.

Anna forgot the rain, her damp clothes, the cold clammy feel of her shoes. She was totally absorbed in sensations which were too new to her to be comprehended easily. Happiness, doubts, hope, entangled inextricably inside her.

The *auberge* was shuttered and in darkness as they approached, but further along the narrow village street they saw a sudden gleam of light, heard voices. The guard had found the wheelwright, clearly.

Charles rapped on the door of the *auberge*. They heard loud grumbling, then a window opened above, and a voice called out to know their business.

Charles explained. The other passengers were already in earshot. The querulous voices of the women carried through the air, complaining of the rain.

"I will be down directly," the landlord promised, his wary suspicion changing.

Soon they were in a small, dusty room, watching the landlord throwing fresh wood on to the smoldering ash fire. A short, dark woman bustled to and fro, preparing hot soup, attending to the other ladies, removing their bedraggled outer clothes, soothing and reassuring them. Candles gave the room a spurious homeliness.

The elegant young man spread his damp coat-tails at the fire, sighed with content at being out of the rain again.

"Those two old hens clucked at me every inch of

the road," he whispered to Anna. "I had to walk with one on each arm!"

Anna looked up at him, eyes dancing. She tried to smother the answering twinkle, but could not quite manage it, and for a moment they smiled at each other in amusement.

"I'm sure you were very gallant," she told him.

He looked admiringly at her. Despite her muddy skirts and wet, wind-whipped hair, she looked charming. Her cheeks had a warm pink glow in the candlelight, and her eyes were a dark, shining blue beneath those long lashes.

Charles entered the room suddenly. The young man started, mumbled a word of excuse and hurriedly left.

"You must be careful," Charles drawled, dark brows raised. "You seem to have attracted an admirer."

"Why not?" she shrugged.

"We do not want to be drawn into intimacy with strangers," he murmured, leaning down so that she could just hear the words. "I am afraid you must curtail your charming flirtation."

"I was not flirting!"

"No?"

"I could hardly ignore him when he spoke, could I?" She found it hard to keep her voice down, her anger kept rising inside her.

"You were fluttering your lashes and smiling invitingly," Charles said softly.

Their eyes met with the angry sheen of daggers. A small muscle twitched at the corner of his mouth. Amusement, she wondered? Mockery? Or was it really anger she saw in that fierce, dark face, an anger that seemed to echo the bitter rage she had seen the first time they met, when he took her for Maria?

There was a brief flash of hope once more as she realized all that his anger could mean. Jealousy of her? She looked at him carefully, then away, sighing. Between them still lay the shadow of his brother, of Maria's cruelty.

"You seem remarkably casual, considering the dangers we are running," he whispered. "Remember, we have a long way to go before we are safely over the border."

A flicker in the doorway made Anna turn. She saw a back, broad and damp with rain, disappear into the corridor. Her nerves leapt. Charles followed her gaze.

"Who was it?"

"The other man from the coach," she whispered, her voice a little shaky.

"Was it, by God?" Charles bit his lip. She could see that he was wondering just how much, if anything, the other had overheard of their conversation.

"We were speaking very low," she reminded him anxiously.

"I hope it was low enough," he snapped.

The other guests were coming back into the room to eat the supper prepared for them. The landlady was deftly carrying in the odorous broth, followed by a sleepy, smear-aproned girl carrying bread and cheese.

They sat around the table, eating in a silence only broken by a complaint from one of the thin women. Once Anna looked sideways, uneasily, and found the sturdy merchant watching her from beneath half-lowered lids. Her spoon jarred against her bowl. Charles looked at her quickly. Her eyes desperately signaled her alarm. He looked away without response, yet she knew he had read her silent message accurately.

She was relieved when it was possible to rise from

the table and leave the room. The landlady had, she found, put her into the same room as the two thin sisters. Her bed was lumpy and very uncomfortable. She suspected the sheets to be alive with vermin, but she was too tired to care. She took off her gown and hung it over the end of the bed. Her petticoats were stiff with mud at the hem. A fine mess I must look, she told herself without really caring.

She was asleep within ten minutes, and only woke in the gray dawn light when she heard the loud rattle of wheels outside the window, and knew that somehow the wheelwright had contrived to make the coach roadworthy once more.

The sisters stirred, in the bed they shared, and sat up, exclaiming. Anna bade them good-morning and received polite smiles. Their relief had done wonders for their tempers, she saw.

They were on their way within an hour, warm, refreshed and well fed, and even pleased to be rumbling slowly along the rutted roads once more. The air was cool and moist. The earth, sodden with rain, seemed to steam gently as the sun came out. Craters in the road were like small lakes, reflecting for them the pale moving sky and the leafless trunks of trees.

"So you are going to Dijon," the handsome young man murmured to Anna as they progressed.

All the passengers seemed more talkative this morning. Their night's adventure had brought them together, given them an illusion of a danger shared, a common past.

"Yes," she admitted, unguardedly, and at once felt Charles stiffen, and was aware that the other passengers, too, were all listening.

Was it her imagination, or did she sense more than the usual curiosity in their stare?

"But you are not from Dijon," came the young man's reply, and his smile teased her. "I was born there. I would remember you if I had ever seen you before!"

"You were born there? Then you are going home?" She managed to reply without answering the implied question of where she did come from.

"Going home," he agreed, and went on to talk of his cousin, who was a prominent citizen; a member of the revolutionary committee, a lawyer of some note. His voice held pride, affection.

Anna froze. He had not mentioned his cousin's name during this eulogy, but all these things described Yves Saint-Denis. Of all the men in France he was the last she wished to encounter. He might, before she could warn him, betray her real identity. She felt, remembering Yves, that he would not knowingly betray her, of course, but the risk must be enormous.

"Lawyers!" The thin sisters reacted to the word as though it were a gun. "We were robbed of our inheritance by lawyers!" They burst out with the details of some petty family squabble over a lawsuit in the course of which a large sum had just evaporated.

Anna leant back, listening vaguely. She dared not ask the name of the young man's cousin. The last thing she wanted was to admit acquaintance with anyone in Dijon.

At the next halt she was alone with Charles long enough to warn him about Yves.

"If you had told me," he burst out furiously, "we could have avoided Dijon, but now we must go on or we shall certainly arouse suspicion. Is this man your enemy? Is he a fanatic, likely to betray us?"

She shook her head with certainty. "He is not a fanatic, though he does believe in the revolution. No, he would never betray me." Unguardedly, her tone put emphasis on the last word, and Charles looked at her sharply.

"No?" His eyes were hard and probing.

She remembered her first meeting with them both. It was odd that they should have met like that. She looked at Charles, hesitating, then said, "He is the man who came into the room, that first day, and found us quarreling . . ." Was that mild word a fair description of the violence with which Charles had shaken her, she wondered?

The dark face stiffened, the brows arched. "That fellow?" He stared over her head, then his lips twisted. "He seemed a chivalrous aristo to me, not a bourgeois lawyer . . ."

"There is no need to sneer! Yves is naturally gentle." Then she paused, and frowned. "But . . ."

"But?"

"He might give us up if he decided it was his duty!"

Charles laughed sardonically. "Ah, yes—that would be in his nature! Conscience! A man of conscience . . ." He made the words sound deeply insulting.

Then he looked at her, and saw her anxiety. He shrugged. "Well, we must keep an eye open for him. With luck we shall never set eyes on the fellow."

As they approached Dijon Anna's nerves began to twist like tangled threads. At any moment they could be arrested. She almost wished it would happen, so that it would all be over and done with, and she could stop fighting this pain, this tortured anxiety.

The passengers were all silent now, exhausted by their journey, perhaps, or already thinking ahead, as she was, to their long-awaited destination.

The *diligence* pulled up at the barrier. Anna fidgeted with her hair, her hands shaking. The sturdy merchant suddenly climbed down and walked off. The soldiers guarding the barrier stiffened. Charles leaned forward, watching from the window.

Anna felt her hands tighten. Dampness trickled between her fingers. Her forehead was sticky with sweat. She looked at Charles, eyes wide.

A soldier came towards the coach and opened the door. He beckoned to Charles and Anna, his face impassive.

"Descend and follow me!"

The other three passengers looked at them in mingled alarm and curiosity. Charles stood up. Anna put her hand out, and felt his fingers grip hers, wringing them hard.

Charles looked casually irritated. "What is wrong?" he asked the soldier as they obeyed.

"Silence! You will produce your documents!"

"Some muddle over identity, I suppose," he said to Anna with a careless shrug of annoyance.

The sturdy man at the barrier looked at them both with a cool, stolid expression as they approached. Charles gave him a hard look.

"Information has been given to us," said the officer in charge, with a crisp nod to the soldier. "Where are your papers? Are they in order?"

Charles slowly and without apparent alarm produced their documents. There was a silence while the officer studied them. Anna watched his face nervously, trying to appear as unconcerned as Charles did.

It seemed a very long time before the man looked up. His face was still without expression.

"I am not satisfied with your papers. You will accompany me to the committee rooms to be interrogated."

Charles looked at him in seeming irritation. "Are you telling me we are under arrest, *citoyen?*"

"You are," the officer barked.

Anna sighed and his glance switched quickly to her face. She frowned at him.

"I have had a long journey, *citoyen*. I am tired. Is this the freedom for which we fought on the barricades in Paris?"

The officer shrugged. "These matters have to be investigated. I am sorry."

"What is wrong with our documents?" she pressed, risking everything on a frontal attack.

His face was noncommittal. "I will ask the questions, *citoyenne*. You are under arrest. That is sufficient."

Nine

They were taken to a bare room, under military escort, and left there, alone, with only the slow tramp of the soldiers outside the door to remind them that they were under arrest. Anna, despairing, looked at Charles.

"What will happen, do you think?"

He turned his dark eyes on her coolly. "They have no proof of anything, yet—our fellow traveler informed against us, but he could have had nothing but suspicions to convey. He overheard us talking in that damned inn, as I feared."

She shivered. "And at once betrayed us!"

Charles laughed. "How naïve you are—of course he did. He will be well rewarded for his patriotism. Who knows what he wants in exchange—office for himself or a relative, money, power? Men will betray their own brothers to the guillotine for less!"

"But what will they do to us?" She was anxious for him, knowing what must happen if they were sent back to Paris. She might be spared, being English. There was a chance for her. But for Charles there was no chance at all. He would be found guilty of treason, sentenced to a terrible, humiliating, shameful death in front of the half-savage crowds. White-faced, she stared up at his eyes, trembling. She could already see that handsome, arrogant head severed, hear the sickening roar of the crowd as it fell forward.

He caught her by the arms, bending forward. "Where is your courage? Look like that and their suspicions will be doubled. We must try to bluff our way out of here, play for time . . ."

"You could leave me here," she said. "Go on alone—your papers are all in order! After all, I am English. What harm can they do me? They would not dare kill an English subject!"

He laughed contemptuously. "Your faith is pitiful, my dear." He touched the tricolor cockade which, like all travelers, he wore in his hat. "This is all that stands between us and death! We must convince the local revolutionary committee that we are honest French patriots."

Outside the door there was a sudden change in the sound of the military tramping. A salute, a raised voice, then the door was flung open.

Charles turned casually, with no perceptible trace of fear, and looked at the men who entered. Anna, tense and pale, stared too, but as she looked, felt her nerves leap.

One of the men was all too familiar. Quiet, yet with an unstressed authority in his bearing, he wore the black garb and tricolor sash of the revolutionary official.

It was Yves.

Charles shot her a glance, eyes narrowing, as he heard the quickly stifled gasp of half relief, half surprise.

Then he looked again at the newcomers. His eyes

clashed with those of Yves. Recognition showed on both faces.

The other men carried the tools of interrogation—paper, ink, quills. They were clearly subordinate to Yves, who stood slightly in front of the others, his manner guarded.

Anna fixed Yves with burning eyes, willing him not to betray her trust.

His eyes slid over her without a glimmer of response, his face marble in repose.

He looked back at Charles. "We must have met before, *Citoyen* Baccoult."

Charles inclined his head. *"Citoyen* Saint-Denis!"

The other men showed interest. Anna saw them exchange looks, felt an immediate relaxation of the tension which had entered the room with them.

"You do recognize him, then, *citoyen?*" asked one of the others, a tall, hard-faced man with a twisted nose which gave him a brutally ugly expression.

Yves looked round calmly. "But, yes. The *citoyen* doctor is well known in Parisian revolutionary circles. We met while I was there."

"Another wild goose chase!" The speaker was a fat, pompous little man whose tricolor sash was strained tight across his over-abundant paunch.

"And the woman?" The man with the ugly nose looked at Anna. "Is she, too, known to you, *citoyen?"*

Yves once more glanced casually at Anna. "I fancy I saw her in the doctor's company once or possibly twice. I recall someone mentioning a sister." His tone dismissed the subject. "I regret that you have been troubled, Doctor Baccoult, but you understand how it is—one must take it seriously when information is laid against a stranger, particularly in these frontier areas. The borders are sensitive just now."

Charles shrugged. "I understand. You forget, I have a brother serving in the army."

"On what front?" asked Yves quietly.

"I believe he is fighting the invading armies somewhere along our border with the Netherlands." Charles spoke slowly, watching Yves. "Have you heard any recent news?"

"Some good, some bad," Yves said. "You must be anxious about your brother. I will give you all my news over some wine, and then, *citoyen,* you shall give us the news from Paris."

The other men fell back as Yves conducted them out of the bare little room.

Yves took them to his own office. When the other men had gone back to their posts and the door was closed, shutting the three of them safely in the room, he turned to Anna.

"Well, my dear Anna," he said softly. "I have been anxious for you ever since I heard of the arrest of all English subjects. I tried to discover what had happened to you. I had our mutual friends scour the prisons, but they could find no word of you at all. I hoped that you had returned to England somehow. What are you doing here?"

"It is a long story," she said, smiling. After the tension of the last few moments she felt suddenly giddy and sick. She groped for a chair and sat down.

"Are you ill?" Yves crossed to her quickly, but Charles was there before him, kneeling to look into her white face, his hand on her wrist, taking her pulse.

Yves watched them both curiously. Anna's eyes had closed. Their lids had a delicate, bruised look, the blue veins visible against her thin white skin. Charles looked angry, his mouth compressed.

"I am not going to faint," Anna said flatly. Her voice sounded weak, even in her own ears, and she despised herself for her weakness.

Charles made a grimace. "No, I can see you are not. Your obstinacy is infuriating. Why drive yourself so hard? Is it so shameful to feel like a woman now and then, you little English puritan?"

The lids fluttered open. Anna looked down into the dark, brooding face. A tender, rueful smile curved her mouth. "You have a strange manner with your patients, doctor. You treat them with rough impatience."

Charles stood up. "You are better, I think."

Yves looked quizzically at Anna. "My curiosity is mounting, my dear. May I now hear the story of how you come to be in Dijon with the *citoyen* doctor?"

She flushed at the look in his face. "My uncle and I were arrested," she said. "Charles saved us from the Luxembourg, and now he is trying to help me to escape to Switzerland."

"Geneva," Charles said.

Yves scratched his chin. "You know, of course, that Geneva is under French influence at present? There is a strong revolutionary movement there. You will not necessarily be safe even should you reach the Geneva canton safely."

"We will be making for Trieste, eventually," Charles said.

"Ah!" Yves nodded. "Of course, English ships often put in there. You have to get to Trieste first, though. Geneva is so near the border—you could so easily be brought back."

"We have got so far," Charles replied calmly. "I believe we will finish our journey."

Yves stared at him, lifting one eyebrow. There

was a grudging admiration in his face. "I believe you will, too, *citoyen*."

Charles grinned. "And you?"

"I? What should I do? I am a Frenchman, an official of the people, but I am first a man. I shall say nothing, do nothing." He looked into the other man's face, his gaze direct. "Be good to her."

Charles held his gaze, his face thoughtful. He nodded.

"Yves," said Anna, distressed, "do you not understand how much he has done for me? He has sacrificed his life, his career, his family. He is going into exile! I shall never be able to repay him for his courage and generosity."

Charles moved in a restless, angry way, his eyes fierce on her. "You talk in a tiresome way, *citoyenne*. I want to hear no more." He looked at Yves. "What are our chances of getting through the border?"

Yves shrugged. "That depends on luck." He smiled. "You seem plentifully supplied with good fortune so far—I hope your luck holds."

Teeth tight with determination, Charles said, "It must. It shall."

They were on their way again an hour later. Charles, a little curtly, refused an offer of money from Yves, and Yves did not press him, shrugging. While Charles was talking to the postilion of the coach they had hired to take them into Switzerland, Yves took Anna's hand in both of his and looked regretfully at her.

"I wish you had written to me. I would have come back to Paris at once."

"Everything happened so fast. I had no time to think."

"Would you have sent for me if you had thought of it?" he asked, watching her carefully.

She looked at him frankly. "No. I had no claim on your kindness, Yves."

His mouth tightened. "You love that fellow. I knew it from the first day I saw you together. My instincts were accurate."

She shook her head. "I had only just met him that day. I was telling you the truth, Yves."

"It can happen like that," he said flatly. "A glance is enough, sometimes. I could sense it between you, like a glove thrown down in challenge."

"He hated me," she said. "He probably still does."

"You do not believe that."

She sighed so that her body trembled. "Sometimes I do—I see contempt and hatred in his eyes. At other times I . . ."

"Hope?" he probed gently.

Her silence answered him.

He stared at her averted face, watching the fluttering lashes, the compressed lips which reined in another deep sigh.

"I wish you had given me the right to protect you," he said, in a deep voice. "It wrenched me in half to leave you in Paris. If I had been aware of your uncle's folly, of the risks you would be running so soon, I would have taken you away, willing or not."

She half laughed, half sobbed. "Would you, Yves?" Her lids rose and they looked at each other for a moment, silently.

He shrugged again. "I am a fool. I hope you get what you want, Anna, although I cannot believe that Baccoult will make you happy."

Charles returned. His narrowed eyes rested on them, standing so intimately together. Then Yves drew away from her and Anna turned towards Charles.

"Are we ready?"

"I am ready," he said, with a snap. "Are you?" His glance challenged them both, suspicious and fierce.

"Yes," she said meekly. She lifted her face towards Yves, a smile on her lips but the faint moisture of tears in her eyes.

Yves took her hands, kissed them gently and released them. He pulled her cloak closer around her throat.

"You have far to go. Look after yourself."

"And you, Yves," she whispered. The ambiguous, understated words seemed to beat inside her head, like the muffled roll of drums before an execution.

For so long, friends had vanished overnight, without warning. Yves seemed safe enough, but the last year had taught her how insecure the future could be, how rapidly circumstances could change.

"Dijon is not Paris," said Yves below his breath. "But I walk warily, *chérie*. I know the traps which line the path, the wild beasts lurking in the undergrowth. With a little luck, I shall avoid the worst."

She leaned out to wave, for as long as she could see him, the tears running down her face. Then she sank back against the seat, meeting the dark and somber stare with which Charles regarded her. His eyes were cruel, filled with their old enmity.

"How touching a sight!"

"Don't sneer! I hate it when you speak in that voice."

"We *petit bourgeois* cannot help ourselves," he said, in the same cold, drawling tone. "Our low birth betrays us!"

She moved restlessly, turning her head away. Why had she been fool enough to fall in love with this man who was now looking at her with bitter hatred? Why could she not have fallen in love with someone kind and gentle, like Yves?

From Dijon they took the road into the green foothills of the Jura, a road which, at first, ran through the fertile vineyards of Burgundy, passing peaceful villages where it seemed impossible to believe that the horrors of Paris existed. The journey was slow and uncomfortable, broken with frequent halt for change of horses and meals.

As they came nearer the Swiss border the horses slowed to a walking pace, taking the steep roads with difficulty, and from time to time Charles and Anna got out and walked alongside the carriage to lighten the load and stretch their legs.

Above them rose the dark, pine-forested slopes, now and then divided by a clear, tumbling stream of icy water which ran down the limestone rocks and filled the valley rivers.

"A majestic prospect," Charles said, gazing upwards. The sky, blue and pristine, made a fitting backcloth.

They met little other traffic on the road. A few peasants, walking with donkeys or on mules, passed them, stared incuriously and grimly ignored their greeting.

"Not a very friendly people in these parts," Anna said.

"Most people are wary of getting involved with strangers since the revolution," Charles shrugged.

They had hoped to reach the border before dusk on the second day after leaving Dijon, but the unexpectedly bad state of the roads made their progress much slower than they had expected and dusk fell while they were still toiling up one of the steep mountain pass roads.

They had dismounted, to ease the strain on the weary horses, and Anna found it difficult to see where she stepped, in the soft, thickened dusk. The pine-scented air filled her lungs, cold and fresh, backed by a wind which seemed to come from far up in the mountains.

Suddenly, from lower down the trail behind them, they heard the muffled sound of hoof beats. A scrape of a horse's shoe on rock, the panting of a rider, and then, against the gray-purple bloom of the sky, a figure was outlined, coming round a bend in the road.

Anna clutched at Charles's arm, her fingers tightening on him. Her heart pounded sickeningly.

Charles halted and watched the approaching rider, tense yet coolly poised.

The carriage toiled forward. The driver glanced back, as surprised as they were to hear some other traveler upon the road at that hour.

Then the rider was upon them, looking down. He was tall, very thin, dressed in black, with the tricolor fluttering in his hat.

Before either of them could greet him he had drawn a pistol from his coat and leveled it at them. Anna's breath caught in her throat. Was he a thief, or an official of the Republic?

Calmly, Charles said, "What is this, citizen?"

Anna could only see half of the newcomer's face. The upper part of his features was hidden by the shadow of his hat. His jaw was long and sharp, his lips thin. They twitched now into the mockery of a smile, shafted down at them like a weapon, bitter with malice.

"Sir Henry's arrival in England is known in Paris, citizen. I have been sent, post haste, to see to it that you, at least, do not escape the vengeance of the French people."

Anna was amazed by the coolness with which Charles took this threat. Her terrified glance saw no fear in his handsome face. He seemed almost to shrug. "Are you an actor, citizen? What melodrama do you offer us?" His tone was lazily acid.

The other man laughed softly, yet indefinable menace emanated from him. He leaned forward slightly, resting the hand that held the pistol upon his saddle. The leather creaked and Anna realized, by the silence, that the carriage had come to a halt, and the driver was staring back at them, curious but unwilling to get involved in whatever was afoot. Men had quickly learnt to steer clear of such involvement. She could not blame him.

"Do not fence with me, Citizen Baccoult—I have ridden across France without stopping for three days. I have had half a dozen fresh horses. I badly need sleep—if you irritate me, I warn you, my finger might slip upon the trigger, and that I would regret, since my superiors are very desirous of seeing you mount the steps of the guillotine."

Charles shrugged again. "What am I supposed to have done? With what crime am I charged?"

"We know, Baccoult, we know!" The other man's voice was still softly malicious. "The traffic between France and England is a dual affair—we get news from England daily. Sir Henry had but set foot on English soil when the word was sent back to Paris. You are lucky to have got so far—it was only due to a slight disagreement within the government. Some people were afraid that Sir Henry's successful escape, if publicly acknowledged, might be embarrassing."

Charles laughed. "Oh, I imagine it will cause some amusement in royalist circles, yes!"

The other man's lips drew back in a snarl. "So! You're a damned royalist, are you?"

At that moment the horses pulling the carriage grew restless and moved suddenly, their feet sliding on the rocky path. A few stones rolled down, rattling, and the horseman instinctively turned his head to look at them.

Charles leapt at him, in that second, and Anna, terrified that he would be killed, bent and snatched up a large stone from the grass, hurling it at the horseman's head in a reflex action as she straightened.

It struck him full upon the head and he plunged forward and down from his horse. At the same instant, though, his pistol discharged and Charles staggered back.

"Charles!" she screamed in despair. "Oh, Charles, no!"

The two bodies lay together, entangled. Anna knelt beside them, pushing the heavy limbs of the stranger away so that she could lift Charles's head.

The dusk gave her only the dim outline of his white face. Her tears dropped down on to his cheek as she held his head cradled against her breast.

"He's not dead," she sobbed, as though half pleading, half threatening fate. "He can't be dead!" Her free hand explored his face, head, shoulder, searching for the wound that had felled him. Then she froze, feeling a wetness on his fingers.

She lifted her hand and stared at it. A dark stain covered her palm.

"Oh, God!" She moaned. But where was the wound, and how serious was it?

She looked round desperately for help. The driver stolidly stood beside the stationary carriage, watching.

"Help me!" she called to him. "Bring your lantern! He is wounded!"

The driver spat upon the ground, paused, then climbed upon his seat once more, whipped up his horses and rattled slowly away in the direction of the frontier.

He had gone to call out the frontier guards, she thought. Now they were in the last trap. It was all over.

Ten

Crouching over Charles, still silently crying, she began again to feel for the betraying stain which would identify the nature of his wound.

Suddenly he moved, faintly, and her heart pounded with joy and relief.

He looked up at her, dazedly. "What?"

"He shot you," she whispered. "Are you in much pain?"

He moved again, sitting up, and winced, touching one arm with his other hand.

"My left arm," he murmured. "Fortunate! It could have been worse!" Then he looked round rapidly, stared at the other dark form lying so close to them, then at the empty road where the carriage had stood.

"How did he come there?"

"I threw a stone at him," she said. "Just as he fired at you."

Charles laughed. "Help me up!"

She did so, gently, supporting him with both arms. He looked down, bent and picked up the pistol.

"Best take this with us! Our driver ran away, did he?"

"He will be back with soldiers, I am afraid," she

said. "He heard what that man said to you, you know . . ."

Charles nodded. "We are only a few miles from the border here. We must cross the long way round . . ." And he pointed upwards, to where the pine trees moved sighing in the night wind.

"Can you manage to climb with a wounded arm?"

"It is only a flesh wound. When we dare rest a while, I'll have you bind it up. For now, we must hurry. There's no time to waste if we are to escape."

They moved carefully upward, between the pines, sending stones clattering down despite their care. Each sound made her wince in imagined dread. She strained for sounds of pursuit, but when she looked back could only see the dark valley below them, and the darker shape of a horse contentedly cropping from the grass at the roadside. Somewhere nearby, she knew, the body of that man must lie. Her blood chilled as she wondered if she had killed him.

Charles glanced down, leaning against the rough trunk of a pine.

"What is it? You are trembling."

"Nothing," she said, her voice quivering involuntarily.

"Frightened?" His tone was gentle.

"No. Now . . . no. I was—for a while, down there, when I thought you were dead."

He put his free hand to her hair in a half tender gesture. "Were you?"

Her heart quickened, then she thought again of that man, of the thud of the stone against his head, of the way he had fallen forward, suddenly heavy and limp.

"Do . . . do you think I killed him?" she asked Charles weakly.

"Is that what is worrying you?" He laughed. "He was still breathing when I took his pistol, my dear."

Her long sigh made him laugh again. "We must not delay any longer," he said, and began to climb again, with her close beside him.

The scent of the pines, the increasing chill in the air, filled her lungs with invigorating cold. She pulled her cloak around her, then wondered how long Charles could go on without tiring. The loss of blood must be weakening him.

"When shall we be able to stop, so that I may see to your wound?" she asked.

"Wait," he panted. "I want to put a good way between us and all pursuit."

When he thought they had climbed high enough, he began to work his way to the west, towards the lakeside. After some time he halted and slid slowly down towards the ground. A carpet of pine needles, and the acid smell of damp earth rose to her nostrils as she knelt beside him.

He winced as she dealt with his wound, deftly. In the darkness she could only bind it with a strip of linen torn from her petticoat. It was, he said, only a flesh wound. Fortunately the ball had not been embedded in his arm, and the bleeding had done something to cleanse the wound.

Charles lay back for a moment, eyes closed. Above them the night sky was full of stars. The moon came out briefly, then passed behind a cloud, but Anna had seen Charles in that second, had recognized the deadly weariness in his features, the pallor and the lines of pain etched around his mouth.

When, after a while, he struggled to his feet, she protested. "Can we not sleep here? They will not look for us, surely, among these mountains?"

"We must cross into Switzerland before dawn," he said tautly. "Once it is light enough to see, it will be too risky. We must move on now . . ."

They went on slowly, Charles holding his wounded

arm stiffly beside him, and then, below them, there came the bright gleam of water under the stars.

Pinpoints of light glittered upward from the waves blown up by the wind. Charles paused, breathing heavily.

"A beautiful sight . . . Lake Geneva . . ."

"Switzerland," she murmured, in mingled relief and anxiety. "How shall we know when we are in Switzerland?"

Charles laughed. "Wait until we are in the city itself, my dear . . . once we reach the safety of your friend's house we can relax . . ."

From somewhere, far behind and below, they could hear voices and the sound of movement. A lantern gleamed briefly, a mile or so back, along the frontier road, as though one of the stars had fallen from the sky.

"They are searching for us . . ." Charles said. "We must move on . . . We have the advantage for the moment, but it only needs one more stroke of bad luck for us to be caught . . ."

Their way lay downward now, towards the lake, and as they climbed lower their progress grew faster.

They struck a road, at last, and hovered, in the shelter of some trees, watching and listening. A cart came rumbling along, pulled by a raw-boned old horse. The driver, a hunched peasant, had his head down on his chest, as though asleep, swaying to the movement of the cart.

Charles stepped out on to the road, the pistol leveled. "Halt!" His voice was low but firm.

The peasant jerked upright and reined in his horse, staring at the weapon.

"Are you taking those vegetables to Geneva?" Charles demanded.

The man nodded, still hypnotized by the pistol.

Charles motioned to Anna. "Climb into the back."

Then, to the man, with quiet menace, "Now, my friend, take us to Geneva and do not make any foolish moves or you will find yourself with a hole in your back . . ."

"Are you French?" the peasant asked, as he clicked at his horse.

"What if we are?"

"Refugees?"

"What difference to you?"

"You are in Switzerland now, you know," the peasant said. "We are a law-abiding people. We don't like having pistols pointed at us . . ."

"Keep driving," Charles said. "How far to the city?"

"Half a mile. They won't cross the border to take you back, you know. You are quite safe."

"I shall feel safe when I am well into Switzerland," Charles said.

They reached the house of the MacAndrew family early that morning. A footman opened the door, his lofty glance skimming the tops of their heads.

"Yes?" The hauteur of his tone made Charles glare at him.

"Mademoiselle Campbell," he said icily.

"Not at home . . ." the footman said, beginning to shut the door. Charles blocked the doorway with his foot.

"Inform Mademoiselle that her cousin has arrived from France," he snapped.

The footman hesitated, glancing at Anna, then allowed them to pass him. "Please wait in this room," he said stiffly, opening a door off the hall and showing them into a small chamber.

"Your arm is giving you pain," Anna said anxiously, looking up at Charles. "I wish you had agreed to have it properly dressed before we came here . . ."

"When I have given you into the care of your cousin I shall take my leave," he said curtly.

Her eyes stung with unshed tears. He would go away and she would never see him again. She could hardly bear to contemplate a future in which he had no part.

The door suddenly burst open, and Feuvielle hurried in, his face full of a surprisingly genuine emotion.

"My dear Anna!" He caught her by the shoulders as she rose, smiling at her. "You are alive! Is it possible? We had given up all hope . . . news came that you were dead, both of you . . ." Then he looked at Charles, and a startled, puzzled expression filled his eyes. "Not Sir Henry?" He looked back at Anna. "Where is your uncle, then?" His eyes narrowed in alarm. "Is he, after all, dead?"

"No," she assured him. "No, truly—he is alive and well. In England now. He escaped by fishing boat—the fishermen would not take me." She looked behind him, at the open door. "But where is Maria?"

"She will be down in a moment," Feuvielle said. "I left her getting dressed."

Anna's eyes widened in shock. A flush burned her cheeks. "You what?"

He laughed, his slanting eyes meeting hers in that old, mocking, intuitive comprehension.

"We were married a week since—when we received news from France that made me believe it would be impossible to wait for Sir Henry's permission. Maria needs protection, and I could only give it if she was legally my responsibility." His amused, intimate glance flitted from her to Charles. "You know Maria, my dear! She has been causing havoc in Geneva. The sooner we get her to England the better for the Swiss!"

Maria rustled into the room, fluttering, beautiful, wide of eye and elegantly tearful.

"Dearest, dearest Anna!" She embraced her cousin with an emotional gesture while, with half-closed lids, she surveyed Charles in curious disbelief.

Soon she was seated beside Anna, on an elegant striped sofa, listening to the tale of their escape with bated breath. Her husband, lounging lazily on the opposite side of the room, watched her with all his old, cynical, amused, tolerant understanding.

Charles rose, after a while, and made a polite excuse, but Feuvielle would not hear of his leaving the house until he had met their hosts, who were all still abed.

"I am sure they will wish to offer their thanks for your gallantry and courage, as my wife and I do," Feuvielle drawled.

"Could a doctor be sent for?" Anna asked anxiously, reminding them of the wound to Charles's arm.

"But of course!" Feuvielle rang the bell, and dispatched the supercilious footman for the nearest doctor.

That evening they dined *en famille* with the Mac-Andrew family. Their adventures were the major topic of conversation. Mrs. MacAndrew was a grayhaired woman with a capacity for astonishment which was almost a virtue in her since she spoke so rarely, and with such phlegmatic calm normally, that she barely seemed to have any personality at all, apart from her air of continual astonishment. Her husband was a tall, hawk-nosed Scot with stately manners, who showed Anna great courtesy, and seemed overjoyed by his old friend's safe return to England.

He took Anna aside, after dinner, to explain why

he had consented to Maria's marriage, and to inquire anxiously as to Sir Henry's possible reaction.

"Feuvielle seemed suitable enough," he murmured. "And he had a warm letter of recommendation from Henry . . . I did it for the best." A look of embarrassment crossed his face. "Maria had a tendency to . . . she is . . ."

Anna understood him. He and his wife had been horrified at the prospect of being left with Maria on their hands, outshining their own plain daughters and disrupting their lives by her frivolous, selfish pursuit of pleasure.

Quickly she assured him that her uncle would not disapprove of the match.

"He always approved of Feuvielle," she said.

Mr. MacAndrew looked heartily relieved, and led her back to join the others with a cheerful air. Feuvielle, watching them, showed Anna, by the mocking amusement of his glance, that he guessed very well what had passed between them.

Anna looked across at Maria, who was flirting with Charles on a sofa. A stab of intolerable jealousy pricked at her heart. Charles was smiling at her beautiful cousin. The candlelight gave his pallor a romantic interest, emphasized by the black curls and slanting dark brows. Maria was clearly enjoying herself.

How could Charles, of all people, fall for that spurious sweetness; the false, cloying smiles which Maria offered like counterfeit coin to every attractive man she met?

When, shortly afterwards, Charles rose and began to make his farewell, Mr. MacAndrew hastily begged him not to consider leaving the house that night.

"We had a room prepared for you, sir. I would feel vastly hurt if you left my roof. Sir Henry, my dear old friend, would undoubtedly think me very remiss if I did not pay you every attention possible. The debt we all owe you is beyond repayment, of course, but allow us, I beg you, to do what little lies within our power."

Charles permitted him to proceed, in his stately way, listening with an expressionless face. Then he bowed. "You are very kind, sir, but I must refuse, I think, to take advantage of your generous hospitality. I, too, have friends in Geneva, under whose roof I shall spend the night, as I planned."

Mr. MacAndrew gave Anna an urgent glance. "Really, sir," he protested courteously but firmly, "you must not think of leaving this house yet. Miss Anna, you will support me!"

Quietly she said, "I hope you will stay, sir."

Charles turned his head and looked at her, the dark eyes narrowed.

Her cheeks glowed but she held her gaze steady. "You look pale and tired, sir. I am sure you must be as weary as I am. I mean to retire now, myself."

Mrs. MacAndrew clucked her tongue. "I cannot think how I can have been so blind. Why, child, you are quite wan . . ." And, ringing for a servant, she fussed over Anna, leading her up to her chamber.

Feuvielle, his eyes amused, watched as Maria prettily pouted at Charles, adding her pleas to those of the others.

Charles capitulated, at length, politely accepting the offer of hospitality, yet with such coolness that Feuvielle was curious.

In their own room later, watching his beautiful wife preen herself before her mirror, he murmured softly, "Now, I wonder, what exactly lies between your cousin and her gallant friend?"

And Maria, opening her big eyes wide, said, half in jealousy, half in disbelief, "You think Anna has compromised herself in traveling alone with him?"

Her eyes narrowed. "He is a very handsome young man, it is true."

Feuvielle bent to kiss her naked white shoulder, his smile mocking. "Keep those acquisitive little claws out of him, *ma chère*. I fancy he belongs to your cousin."

Maria tossed her head. "Are you jealous?" she asked, with interest.

Her husband laughed, bringing an angry flush to her face. "Jealous? Silly child . . ." His eyes met hers, taunting her, assured and indifferent.

Maria bit her lip. Despite their marriage, she still found him incomprehensible, and, since she could not be certain of her power over him, she could not afford to relax her watchful jealousy, and this uncontrollable emotion was, for the first time in Maria's frivolous life, forcing her to think of another rather than herself. If she could only once be sure that Feuvielle felt more than an amused indulgence, she would feel free to torment him, as she had so many other men, but he eluded her still, and still she pursued him, with hungry, angry passion.

"Oh," she said now, her voice rising. "Why did you marry me, if you care so little for me?"

He laughed, fondling her expertly, bringing a breathless expectation to her body. "Why, you're a pretty creature, my dear, and I was sorry for you, left so alone in the world . . ."

"Sorry for me?" Her tone rose higher in baffled fury and humiliation.

Feuvielle lifted her in his arms and carried her, struggling furiously, to the great bed. She struck up at him, spitting like a cat, and, as he swooped down over her, he laughed again, before the slow sensuality of his kiss silenced and tamed her, making her, as she angrily recognized, far more his slave than he would ever be hers.

When Anna came down, next morning, she was informed that Charles was feverish and lay abed, at the doctor's insistence. His wound was inflamed, and bodily exhaustion had finally caught up with him.

It was several days before Charles was fit enough to come downstairs. Anna prepared, and sent up, some thin gruel, which was all the doctor would allow. The servants reported, with wooden features, that Charles refused to eat it, and demanded something more filling. Anna sent up thinly sliced veal in a delicate sauce, and had the satisfaction of hearing that Charles had eaten heartily.

Mrs. MacAndrew stolidly remarked that the young man could not be so very ill if he was capable of eating well.

When, at last, Anna saw Charles again she found herself quite breathless as she made her curtsy.

He, wearing his dark clothes with all his old carelessness, bowed jerkily in response, and assured her that he was very well now.

"Will you not be seated?" She looked towards the striped sofa, then took a seat a little away from him.

"Your cousin is out, I understand? And the MacAndrews? I had hoped to have the opportunity of bidding them farewell . . ."

"Farewell?" Her voice shook dangerously.

"I cannot stay here longer," he said. "I must make plans for my future . . ."

Anna struggled with herself. "Of course . . ."

Charles looked at her sharply. "You are very pale! Are you well?"

"Yes!" Despite herself, she snapped, and at the same time felt tears burning behind her lids.

He crossed the room swiftly and bent to take her pulse. She snatched her wrist away.

"Don't!"

The dark features glowed with passionate anger. "Is my touch so intolerable?"

"Yes," she whispered, her head bent.

He pulled her out of the chair, holding her shoulders with fingers that dug into her flesh. The angry face bent towards her, dominating and bitterly passionate.

With a smothered sob she surrendered to his kiss, her hands clinging shamelessly to his shoulders, her knees giving way in an excess of weakness.

When he at last drew back she clung still, her eyes shut tight, the tears running down her face.

"Je t'adore . . ." He cupped her wet face in both hands. "But how can I ask you to be my wife? I cannot provide the luxury to which you are accustomed. An exiled doctor, penniless, with only his hands to earn him a living . . . It would be shameful to ask such a sacrifice of you."

"Charles, I love you," she whispered. "What would I sacrifice? I am not rich. I am a poor relation, dependent upon charity for my bread. Do you think I am afraid to work, to run your house for you? I love you!"

"I am not sure I have the right to accept your adorable generosity," he said anxiously.

She looked up at him and the expression in her eyes made him catch his breath.

He kissed her again, lingeringly, and she slid her arms around his neck to clasp the black curls.

Later, as they sat together on the sofa, he talked of the life they would lead in London. He planned to set up in practice among the many French exiles. They would be able to visit her uncle from time to time.

"Will he hate me for stealing you away from him? I am taking advantage of you, *ma chère . . ."*

"He will be grateful to you for all you have done

for us," she assured him. Her face glowed. "It will be so exciting, Charles—finding a house, setting up home together . . . a new life for both of us!" Her eyes softened. "I hope you will not too bitterly regret leaving France! I hope you will come to like England!" Her mouth trembled. "England! I can hardly believe I shall soon be home again! Wait until you see it, Charles . . . so green and peaceful . . ."

He watched her, smiling. "I think I fell in love with you on that first day," he said, in thoughtful amusement. "The violence of my anger increased the moment I set eyes upon you . . . I felt the tug of attraction, and I resented it bitterly."

She laughed. "And now?"

He pinched her chin. "Madame Impertinence! Now, as you very well know, I am fathoms deep in love, and have ceased to struggle. I find my captivity enchanting."

Anna's eyes danced. "We must remember to thank Maria! I never thought to feel gratitude towards her for her callous nature, I must admit!"

"Yes," he said, soberly. "Had it not been for her cruelty to my poor Louis, we would never have met. I still find it hard to be civil to her, but you will see how I shall try! I mean to work hard at pleasing your family . . . even your damnable cousin-in-law!"

"Feuvielle? I always distrusted him," Anna said slowly. "But now . . . do you know, I rather like him?"

Charles grimaced. "I cannot say I do! I find his cynicism maddening."

"He will make Maria a very good husband, I think. He seems to know how to manage her, far better than my poor uncle did!"

"Your cousin should have a whipping every morning until she learns how to behave!" Charles said.

Anna laughed. "You must suggest it to Feuvielle! It would amuse him, I think!"

Charles laughed. "No doubt! He would not take the advice though!"

"Shall I be whipped, Charles?" she asked teasingly.

He bent to kiss her, his eyes passionate. "Ferociously, if you ever look at another man!" he promised.

THE RELUCTANT DEBUTANTE

*A DELIGHTFUL NEW
REGENCY ROMANCE BY*
MAGGIE GLADSTONE
THE FIFTH BOOK OF THE
LACEBRIDGE LADIES SERIES

Felicia, the youngest—and loveliest—of the five Lacebridge sisters, was certain to make a glittering debut into society. She would be sought after by the most eligible men in London.

Cornelius Tremaine clearly was not among their ranks. He was witty, but his manners were appalling. He was handsome, but his morals were an outrage. There were suitors of greater wealth, greater position and, most certainly, better reputation. Yet as Felicia fell under the spell of this dazzling rakehell, virtue no longer seemed to matter...

Felicia had gone off to sit by herself in a little room at the rear of the house where she could gaze out into the mew behind the house. It was, for the moment, as peaceful a scene as could be found in London, and it did not intrude upon her thoughts.

It was perfectly obvious to her that Ned was no longer the good company she had found him to be back in Wiltshire. Since he had taken on the duty of His Grace's secretary, he had become a stranger to her, so intent upon his labors that nothing else mattered. She herself was as nothing to him. That was a disappointment to her, but, oddly enough, she was not particularly shocked by it, nor did she feel hurt—only annoyed. It meant that her situation at Chalmers House was in no way changed. She still remained without company suited to her.

Now that Emma was expecting, she was sure that her sisters would exclude her from their conversations as never before—and she could hardly expect to be attended by Charles and Ashley. As for Brent, he was the Duke, and he was not the sort of person to spend hours on end in idle chatter, unless it was with Her Grace, Jane.

She smiled at the thought. It was so romantic to see Brent and Jane together. They always appeared to be enjoying each other, no matter who else was in the room.

Now that was the sort of company she should like and, with Ned having declared himself above such paltry dallying, she had no hope left that her stay in London could be better than a bore.

There had been no gentleman at the party last night to offer a more interesting prospect and she was sure that, from day to day, it was bound to be more of the same. They would be calling upon her for one reason or another and prose on endlessly about doings in the City with which she had little familiarity. Yet she must pretend an interest.

Now she thought she would find herself a book to read and go up to her room until it was time for dinner. She arose and went out towards the great salon where her party had been given. She

1

thought that one of Mrs. Halifax's works might be lying about.

When she came to the sliding doors that closed off the great room, she slipped one open and stepped inside. A glance told her that if the book had been about before, it was not now. His Grace's corps of enthusiastic menials had tidied up the salon. Everything was in its place and the volume she sought was now resting on its shelf in the library, no doubt. She turned to leave but stopped as Sir Cornelius came through the door, crying: "Ah, there you are! Well, I must say you have been leading me a merry chase. I pray you to stop a bit so that we may chat."

"I was about to retire to my room, Sir Cornelius," said Felicia. She was surprised to see a look of disappointment in his eyes.

He said: "Then it was me, not Lord Bryson, whom you wished to avoid meeting."

"I do not know what you mean," she replied with great dignity.

"I saw you dash into the house as we approached, and Mr. Gilson thought it was because of his Lordship's presence."

"I'll have you know I do not dash into anything, and as for Lord Bryson—well, I did not think a meeting with him at this time would have been the pleasantest circumstance."

"Blast you, Felicia, cannot you be civil!" he exclaimed. "Have I the plague that you cannot say a kind word to me?"

Felicia's eyebrows lifted. "Indeed, I had no knowledge that you required my sympathy."

"Sympathy? Hell's bells, all I am asking is that you speak with me."

"Unless my ears deceive me, I assumed that that is precisely what we are doing."

"Do you hate me so that this is the best way you can conduct a conversation with me? You are disdainful to a fault and bellicose beyond bearing."

"In that case, I shall withdraw—"

"No!" he cried, spreading his arms to block her passage. "You shall stay and hear me out!"

Felicia rather deliberately supported her elbow in one hand and her chin in the other, staring at him expressionlessly. In a very dull voice, she replied: "It does not appear that I have any choice in the matter. Well, what would you say to me?"

He opened his mouth to speak, reddened, and shifted on his feet. "I—I don't know how to put it."

"I can hardly believe it. For Sir Cornelius to be at a loss for words is truly beyond belief."

She continued to stare at him in the same unenthusiastic fashion.

"I say, do you have to stare at me that way?" he asked uncomfortably.

She said nothing but did not take her eyes from his countenance.

His lips went tight, but not with anger, as his next words showed. "You are prettier, by far, than Lady Mary!"

Felicia looked startled.

"Well, you are!" he insisted.

"I do not see that the point is worth debating," she responded, wonderingly.

"Quite, but what do I say now?"

"*You* ask *me?*"

"Never think it! You would not tell me if you knew."

"I do not know why I stay to listen to you."

The picture of frustration, Sir Cornelius stood with his hands on his hips and glared at her.

"And I am damned if I know why I even try!"

"Oh, Cornelius, what in heaven's name are you trying to say?" demanded Felicia, quite out of patience. "I cannot imagine why you should be in a rage with me."

"I am not in a rage with you!" he shouted. "It is that damnation brother-in-law who has got me into this!"

"Brent?"

"Yes, my cousin Brent."

"I should think that if you had any complaints to make of His Grace, you make them to him, not to me."

"You do not understand. I specifically asked him how it would be and he said all manner of things, but now that I am to the point, none of it makes any sense."

"Frankly, dear sir, none of *you* makes any sense. I haven't the foggiest notion of what you mean."

"Of course, he could be right after all. He said it would not be any fun if I had not got the right one, but I feel it in my liver, you have got to be the right one."

"What you feel in your liver, sir, is hardly a fitting topic between us. I refer you to a medico—"

"My liver?" asked Cornelius, very puzzled. "What has my liver got to do with anything?"

"Well, it was you who brought your liver up. I do not know why."

"Oh, that! Well, that is just an expression. Of course I do not

3

feel a thing with my liver, don't you know. Fact is, haven't a notion where the bloody thing is—if I've even got one."

Felicia made a face of distaste.

Sir Cornelius was apologetic. "Yes, awful expression that, come to think of it—but, I say, how does one put it when one wishes to express—oh, I've got it. The heart! I feel it in my heart. There, is that better?"

"You have a pain in your heart? Perhaps you have been overdoing things."

"What things?"

"How should I know? It is a pain in *your* heart, not mine," Felicia pointed out.

Sir Cornelius paused and stared blankly at her. He was breathing rather heavily.

Slowly he began to shake his head. "It's no use. If there is a knack to it, I have yet to learn it."

"Cornelius, I do believe you are ill. All this talk of livers and hearts—"

"Felicia, I wish you would not put it that way."

"Either you are ill or you are not. What other way is there to put it?"

"The thing that I am trying to make clear to you, Felicia, is that I am not well practiced in this business, and I am failing to express myself to you the way I wish to."

"You know, Cornelius, there was a time when I thought that, blackguard though you were, you were quite dashing. At the moment, I cannot imagine how Sara managed to find you offensive. I do declare I find you most *in*offensive!"

"*In*offensive!" he cried, now very much angered. "*In*offensive, am I?"

He took a step towards her and grabbed her by the shoulders. "I'll show you inoffensive! Here's inoffensive for you!" And he crushed her close to him, bringing his lips down upon hers.

Felicia was quite startled out of her skin and began to struggle to free herself—for a moment, the moment it took for her to acknowledge to herself that what had occurred was precisely what she had wished. And it was something different from what she had expected!

It was nothing like the pecks that she had exchanged on the sly with Ned Manvers. This was like—like...

For the first time in her life, Felicia was speechless and more than content to remain so.

4